# A GLASTONBURY TALE

*Bernard Pearson*

ISBN 978-1-5272-8722-8

### Other publications

*The Discworld Almanak* (2004)
Terry Pratchett with Bernard Pearson

*The World of Poo* (2012)
Terry Pratchett and Bernard and Isobel Pearson

*The Compleat Ankh-Morpork City Guide* (2012)
Terry Pratchett and the Discworld Emporium

*Mrs Bradshaw's Handbook* (2014)
Terry Pratchett and the Discworld Emporium

*The Compleat Discworld Atlas* (2015)
Terry Pratchett and the Discworld Emporium

*Dovetail* (2018)

As someone who has actually sat for weeks on end in Glastonbury market selling his creations, which included a selection of mystic wands. Bernard knows his way around the fringes, not to say, hems, pleats, and gussets of the 'New Age' industry that is stitched into the very fabric of Glastonbury. It was this experience, amongst others that provided the inspiration for 'A Glastonbury Tale'

The story is set in 1996, a time far enough ago to have a gentle haze of nostalgia, and yet not too prehistoric. We read of an ancient house just outside the town that holds a clutch of old hippies in its stony and dilapidated bosom, as well as ancient secrets, dark deeds, and murder most foul amidst the scent of patchouli oil and joss sticks.

It is also a story about those who peddle nostrums, tell fortunes, and make a living selling dreams and eternal wellbeing. There is a bit of daring do, romance and adventure but more than that it's about the need for friends, especially when you get old. And love, which can sometimes provide all the wellbeing you really need, for free.

## Acknowledgments

In my experience no writer works completely alone. There is always someone you call on to provide those snippets of information that fill up the corners of plot or narrative.

Then there are those who very kindly provide the nuts and bolts of grammar, structure and editing. And in my case a manuscript littered with inconsistencies and spelling mistakes.

But those who also aided and abetted the creation of this story were the proof readers who ploughed through some sixty-five thousand words to offer advice on how well the story read, or not, and put me right on so many details. That was a task of real friendship, grit, and perseverance.

So, in no particular order.

My Editor Jean Tilson, bless her. Who tirelessly worked through a meandering plot with diligence and endless patience. Terry Wright who hunted out the errant comma, grammar, and exactitudes of English as it is wrote.

Pat and Jan Harkin who did read and advise so kindly as did Thomas Redpath, whose advice on Glastonbury was invaluable.

Amanda Cummings of Solid Colour who typeset the thing and me dear chum and partner in crime, Ian Mitchell who created the cover. Proving that if you can't polish a turd, you can wrap it up nicely.

And of course, Isobel. My bestest friend and spouse. Without whom I couldn't have begun to tell this tale, let alone find my socks.

In fact, it was friendship, well above the call of duty from all of these lovely people to whom I owe a debt of gratitude and starring rolls should this book ever be made into a film.

May Wellbeing, celestial harmony and all yer chakras align, and I hope you enjoy my merry tale. It does contain nuts though, so beware.

**Bernard Pearson** – *Somerset 2021*

## Authors note

This book is a work of fiction, but its setting is real: Glastonbury is an ancient market town that floats on the Somerset Levels in southwest England. It has a remarkable history and an extraordinary atmosphere. You may be familiar with it from the music festival of the same name or from its diverse spiritual associations. In any case, it is home to a community that proudly and regularly sticks two fingers up at mainstream Merry Old England.

For more than thirteen centuries, Glastonbury has sheltered the pilgrims, eccentrics, radicals, preachers, nonconformists, libertines, intellectuals, iconoclasts, hippies, hermits, and homeless people who have been fortunate enough to reach it. It has offered many souls protection and liberation from a world that can be cruel to those who are different or think too freely. It's a sort of utopia with gift shops.

Since the first stones were laid in the abbey and indulgences sold to pilgrims both rich and poor, it has also been home to those who take advantage of and prosper from the hopes and beliefs of others. The monks sold miraculous cures and the promise of eternal life in the heavens above. Today's gurus and prophets sell eternal youth and wellbeing through various nostrums and lifestyle enhancements. I have enjoyed writing about this aspect of Glastonbury, having a tilt at the windmills that grind out hollow promises and costly but useless therapies.

Primarily, though, this is a light-hearted tale of murder and villainy. And the need for friends, especially when you get old. And love, which can sometimes provide all the wellbeing you really need, for free.

So, let me take you back to the year 1996, which was 1417 in the Islamic calendar, 2540 to the Buddhists, The Year of The Rat to the Chinese, and Year 25 to Mrs Entwhistle and the People of the Golden Dawn at 14 Railway Mews, Glastonbury.

**Bernard Pearson**

*Wincanton, Somerset*
*April 2021*

*To Ian and Reb who have done so much
to make my life a richer and happier place.*

*Chapter 1*

The old woman flew down the staircase with barely a sound, her purple hair waving in wispy profusion. Voluminous cheesecloth skirts billowed around stick-thin legs encased in bright yellow tights. She looked, thought Mildred, like a butterfly. This illusion was shattered when she ricocheted off a stairlift halfway down and crashed headfirst through the spindles under the banister. The sudden stop broke her neck as efficiently as a hangman's noose and caused the vast number of beads she wore to break free and cascade to the hall below like a sudden shower of multi-coloured rain.

Mildred waited at the top of the stairs, listening carefully. The wall clock ticked, the beads dropped and rolled, but there was no other sound in the house. 'So, I haven't lost my touch,' she thought happily as she donned a pair of washing-up gloves and carefully made her way down to Mrs Meldrum's body. The empty bottles she carried in a large plastic shopping bag made only the softest clanking noises as she moved. Upon reaching the dead woman, she lifted her limp right arm and wrapped the still warm hand around the neck of each bottle in turn. Then she scurried back up the stairs to Mrs Meldrum's room. Once inside, she placed the empties on a dresser behind some large figurines as though an attempt had been made to tuck them out of sight, but where they would easily be found when the police searched the room. She put one in the bottom of the wardrobe, too, 'just for luck'. Then she ran down the stairs and through the hall on soft, soundless, slippered feet to the kitchen—where she disposed of her shopping bag and gloves—out the back door, and around to the summer house.

The Major was still fast asleep, snoring away, bless him. This was partly the result of his regular morning pipe of cannabis, and partly due to the diazepam tablet she had slipped into his hot chocolate when he wasn't looking. Major Dennis was such a creature of habit, as military men so often were. Mildred liked people whose train of thought stayed firmly on the rails. Other people's habits were so useful, especially when combined with coincidence. For example, it was the habit of Galadriel, the owner of Grey Havens, to take Mrs Spottiswood to the market on Tuesday mornings. And Tamika, the housekeeper, was in the habit of taking Mr Bendix for his regular appointment at the chiropodist, which just happened to fall on a Tuesday this month. All of the other residents of Grey Havens were currently on holiday or visiting relations elsewhere, and Doris, the cleaner, had just happened to take this Tuesday off. So there had been no witnesses to Mrs Meldrum's death, and Mildred had a clear alibi provided by the Major, who would surely never admit to having been asleep the whole morning. All there was to do now was wait, and she was good at that. She'd had a lot of practice.

Mildred opened her capacious knitting bag, took out her latest woollen creation, and, needles clacking, once again became Granny Toogood, the person the other residents of Grey Havens believed her to be. On the outside she appeared serene, with bright blue eyes peering out from under curly white hair. Slightly plump, she favoured pale pink or beige clothing, and was always, always knitting. Inside, however, and usually demanding to be let out, was Mildred Thresh, CRO number 45237/b/8, whose psychopathic nature had to be contained within whatever alter ego circumstances provided. Mildred was a convicted murderer who had been listed as a missing person since escaping from a psychiatric facility in November 1981. Since then she had hidden in plain sight, living like a parasitic wasp inside a succession of personalities. Her current incarnation, Granny Toogood, was just another of these humble yet highly effective hiding places: a sweet little old lady, beneath notice and above suspicion.

Of course, Mildred hadn't always been old, but she had always been evil. There were many small creatures limping around in the woods behind her house who could have born witness to this, but no humans had known it until she was 13 and her little brother had run into her room without knocking once too often. Poor little Gregory, he hadn't had a leg to stand on. Well, certainly not once she'd seen to him with her "experimenting" knife. But when Mummy and Daddy had rushed in and made such a fuss, well really, she thought, it had been more or less his own fault. Then it got busier, and just a little messy, until it was all nice and quiet again.

Thus, most of her life had been spent in various prisons of one kind or another. But it hadn't been all bad. She'd met some interesting people and learned a lot. Especially from a fellow inmate whose trial had included much expert testimony about blood spatter and bodily fluids, another who specialised in identity theft, and a third who had some very creative ideas on making bodies disappear. As the decades passed and she refrained from killing anyone, she got moved to facilities that were less and less secure. At the last one, more hospital than prison, she'd been assigned to library duty and discovered *The Lady* magazine. It was like reading a Who's Who of potential victims! So many lonely old dears looking for a companion or skivvy. Usually both in the same person, in fact, and decades of institutional living had taught Mildred many domestic skills, along with something even more important: the ability to hide her true self for extended periods of time.

So, Mildred escaped and for the past fifteen years had specialised in companioning elderly women who had no close relatives or friends. Prior to becoming Granny Toogood, she had been Miss Maureen Bailey, a retired hospital matron. The real Maureen Bailey had been eighty and bedridden, but still formidable. She had not, however, been able to cow Mildred, and bedridden old ladies, no matter how imperious, can still be starved to death.

Posing as Miss Bailey, she had moved to Minehead, staying in a small bed-and-breakfast establishment while looking out for her next opportunity. This had come in the form of Mrs Eileen Toogood, the widow of a bank manager, whom she eventually killed using a fairly standard, traceless asphyxiation method involving the clingfilm originally intended for a Women's Institute Victoria sponge. Mildred had been more than a little disappointed in her 'legacy' this time, however. A few trinkets, some cash, some premium bonds; barely a thousand pounds in total. Fifty-odd years of marriage to a dire, pinstriped beanpole named Cyril and at the end she was barely worth a year's groceries! What on earth were the middle classes coming to? 'Good slippers though', thought, Mildred, smiling down at her feet. Barely worn, and so quiet.

After that, while living in a boarding house near Glastonbury, she had heard about Grey Havens at a funeral tea she had crashed to see if there was a vulnerable widow who needed a bit of company. There wasn't, but a chap was extolling the virtues of this rather unusual group home, and it seemed to Mildred that it might be a suitable place for her to lie low and catch her breath. And so she became Granny Toogood.

The knitting needles moved more slowly as she thought about her first victim at Grey Havens, Louise 'Fatty' Spratt. Was it only three months ago? Mildred had certainly not come here intending to murder anyone, but she had been given a room next to an enormous woman who galumphed around the place morning, noon, and night singing bloody arias from her days in the chorus. 'Well, it's all quiet next door now', thought Mildred, and Louise Spratt was just another fat old lady whose asthma had got the better of her (thanks to Mildred's adroit sabotage of every inhaler and nebuliser the woman possessed). As a bonus, the fatal attack had come when the silly cow was staying with her brother. 'I mean to say', thought Mildred, 'staying with a brother who's a florist when you're as asthmatic as Fatty was!' So there had been no investigation; just a quick death certificate from an overworked GP and then the Bristol Crematorium.

This satisfying reflection was interrupted by a scream, high and strident, rising far above the gonging and clanging of the garden's myriad bells and wind chimes. The scream turned into a wail, then abruptly stopped. Soon after, Mildred heard someone swishing through the long grass towards the summer house. Mixed with the swishing sound was a tinkling noise.

That meant Galadriel. 'Bells in the garden, bells in every bloody room of the house, and bells on her stupid clothes', thought Mildred. She closed her eyes and let her body relax.

Galadriel stepped over the threshold of the summer house (or, as she called it, the ashram). She wore a mass of flowing green robes and rainbow-coloured scarves. Long tendrils of red hair fell in chaotic drifts from a tarnished silver clip. Peering into the gloom she saw the Major sleeping peacefully in his campaign chair. Nearby, her knitting all in a heap in her lap, Granny Toogood was also asleep.

As Galadriel approached, Granny blinked and smiled up at her. 'Is it luncheon?' she asked, her voice gentle, refined, of an earlier age.

Galadriel bent down and, taking one her hands, said, 'There's been a dreadful accident, Granny. Mrs Meldrum has fallen down the stairs.'

'Oh, dear! I'll come with you straight away. I did first aid with the Red Cross some years ago. I may be able to be of some assistance. And I'm sure the Major is very good at splints,' Granny added as she gathered her knitting and started to get up. 'Soldiers have training in that, you know.'

Galadriel gently pushed her back down into her seat and said, 'I'm afraid it's quite serious. I've rung for an ambulance. You stay here and when the Major wakes up, perhaps you could tell him.'

Back in the house, Mrs Spottiswood was standing at the bottom of the stairs, sobbing. Her hands were clasped over her ample bosom and the numerous talismans, crystal pendants, and occult necklaces that adorned it. Her gaze was fixed to where Mrs Meldrum's head protruded from the balusters like some exotic hunting trophy, but without the horns.

Just then Tamika drove up to the open front door and decanted Bert Bendix, fresh from his chiropodist appointment. He shuffled into the large hall on Tamika's arm and was confronted by a distraught Mrs Spottiswood. Seeing the object of her consternation looking down sideways at him caused him to stop in his somewhat unsteady tracks.

'Cor, fuck me!' he bellowed. 'Poor old girl looks like a parrot with its head stuck in its cage. Shouldn't happen to anyone, that.' He then added that he needed to use the lavatory and could do with a smoke.

This caused another wail from Mrs Spottiswood, who had always regarded Bert as at best, uncouth and now unfeeling as well. Tamika shepherded him to the nearby lavatory, told him NOT to smoke and then turning to Mrs Spottiswood suggested she go into the big communal room nearby. Once Bert had emerged, she deposited him with Mrs Spottiswood, promised them both a cup of nice hot tea, and went to find Galadriel while the kettle boiled. She found her employer pacing back and forth in front of the big wide window in her office, drawing heavily on a cigarette.

'I phoned for an ambulance, but I knew it was too late,' said Galadriel. 'It'll be the police next.'

Tamika sighed said she was making tea and left. Galadriel looked at the view through the window. All was green and peaceful in the afternoon sunlight. Grey Havens was a sprawling slate and granite Victorian villa (people who knew about such things called the style 'constipated Gothic'). It stood on several acres of land between small lanes that were no more than green drains on the south side of Glastonbury Town.

Its nearest neighbour was a scrapyard and vehicle breaker's a few hundred yards away behind massive, overgrown hedges.

The house may have been influenced by the Arts and Crafts movement, but it showed few signs of either art or craft. The builder had been a local Somerset man who, although skilled in the working of stone, was not one to pay much heed to plans or drawings. He left all that to his son, a young architect steeped in Arthurian lore who convinced their client (a retired maker of sanitary ware whose much younger wife was into spiritualism) that the mystical realms could be reached if certain ancient principals of structural design were followed. What actually followed was a house built with little thought given to reliable plumbing, modern conveniences, or the comfort of its occupants. Before the project was complete, however, the young architect ran off with the young wife to join a mystic sect in Istanbul. The builder finished the job alone, hoping to eventually get paid from the estate of his client, who had promptly shot himself. It was never conclusively established whether this was due to his wife's infidelity or the thought of spending the rest of his days in such a vile monstrosity of a house.

The fire engine was a mistake. Everybody said that, even the fireman. They had heard an old dear was stuck in some stair railings and, being a retained crew and at a bit of a loose end, they arrived first, siren sounding, blue lights flashing, skidding to a halt in a scatter of shingle that ricocheted off windows and took chips off the parked cars. The ambulance arrived a short while later, making a much slower and far less dramatic entrance. It had lost its way twice and switched off both blue light and siren in embarrassment.

Eventually, a lone police car toiled up the bumpy lane and out got Sergeant Arthur Rickets, a man long in service and short on ambition. His driver and 'aide de camp' was one Adrian Pugh, a keen young PC with an evangelical bent.

Crunching across the gravel and the remains of an unlucky hedgehog, they entered Grey Havens. The large hall was full of fireman sipping tea. Fluttering amongst them was a woman with long red hair and flowing garments whom Rickets knew to be the owner of the place. Halfway up a wide, curving staircase a couple of paramedics were bent over a body. Female, if the clothing was anything to go by, and quite obviously dead. In his experience, nobody survived having their neck bent like that. The firemen looked on with mild interest and, as Sgt Rickets pushed his way through them, uttered sotto voce reminiscences of other scenes they had attended where heads had rolled. Every time someone moved there was a crunching noise and some small, bright object skittered across the parquet floor.

The paramedics stood up when Rickets reached them and, seeing law and order in the shape of the Somerset Constabulary, knew this incident was now one they could wash their hands of. With the briefest of nods, one of them muttered 'life extinct,' then they picked up their bags of kit and left.

'Get their details, Pugh,' Sgt Rickets told his constable, who was hovering behind him.

PC Pugh ran to catch up with the paramedics. Luckily, the police car was blocking their exit, or he would never have caught them. As far as ambulance crews are concerned, sudden deaths are the police's problem. Once those bastards have your name in their report it's only a matter of time before you're called in to give evidence. The driver of the ambulance was an old hand, though, and gave the names and number of the other team on duty that day.

Meanwhile, Sgt Rickets had got the fire crew out of the house. In the silence that followed, he stood and gazed up at the late Mrs Meldrum. Then he walked out to his car and called SOCO and CID. To make it more interesting, and because he hated CID, he was a bit sketchy with the details. Not enough to get him into trouble, but more than enough to drag DI 'Farmer' Franks out of his comfortable office. ('Farmer' not through any agricultural association but because he was a dab hand at planting evidence and reaping the rewards.) The house being a bit hard to find, Rickets posted Pugh at the junction of the main road and went back to the house to seek Galadriel.

She was in the lounge, staring into space and chewing her fingernails, while Tamika attempted to maintain order amongst the residents. Until SOCO and CID arrived no one could move Mrs Meldrum's body or even get up the stairs. This was causing a problem for Mrs Spottiswood in particular. She needed to use her own facilities; the downstairs toilet didn't in any way conform to Feng-Shui and might therefore have serious repercussions on her performance. Also, anyone following Bert Bendix into the lavatory would have an olfactory experience second to none.

The two from the ashram had joined the others. Major Dennis was demanding to be allowed to get to his room so he could access his 'field rations.' These consisted of Smarties, Mars bars, and other confections kept in an old ammunition box for when he got the munchies. Granny Toogood was, as ever, knitting, and waiting her turn for the downstairs toilet. She was nothing like as fussy as Mrs Spottiswood, having endured far worse than a lack of spatial harmony when an inmate of Her Majesty's prisons. But it wasn't only her bladder that had driven her into the house; she wanted to see what the police were doing. As near as she could discover, this was not an awful lot, but CID was only just arriving.

Like Sgt Rickets, DI Franks was near to retirement and all for a quiet life. Unlike Sgt Rickets, who was grizzled but lean, DI Franks had obviously enjoyed too many big, Masonic dinners. His bagman, DS Patrick 'Paddy' Doyle, was in complete contrast not only to these two coppers, but to every other policeman in Glastonbury nick. He was in his early forties, had seen service with the RUC and, as the product of a mixed marriage (Catholic mother, Protestant father), had not had an easy career. Witnessing one death too many and the threats that accompanied it had resulted in his being relocated to Somerset, a move that destroyed his marriage as surely as a bullet would have done. With unruly black hair, unsmiling blue eyes, and a large, muscular frame, he had the look of a hard man, which indeed he was. He was also a very good at his job.

Franks and Rickets greeted each other with civil hostility and accepted a cup of what Galadriel said was tea. Then the SOCOs turned up. These were 'Gloves' O'Rourke (because he was so incompetent that no matter how many prints were left at a crime scene his reports always ended with the conclusion that the perpetrators had worn gloves) and his assistant, Sally Gunnel. 'SOCO Sally', unlike her boss, was bright, diligent, and highly efficient. DS Doyle suggested Mr O'Rourke remain with the other senior members of the team (who were now sitting on garden chairs by the front door, chatting and smoking) and he and Sally would make their reports to them in due course.

While Sally examined the staircase in great detail and took copious photographs, Doyle commandeered Galadriel's office and took statements from everyone. Besides Mrs Meldrum, there had only been two people at home during the incident. One of these was a retired army bloke who had apparently been stoned out of his mind, the other an old granny who had been knitting all morning when she hadn't been asleep. According to them, they hadn't actually been inside; they were in some sort of hut in the garden.

When Doyle finished, he joined Sally on the stairs.

'The carpet certainly isn't new,' she told him, 'but I can't see anything to cause a trip. She hit the stairlift when she fell. That thing looks practically homemade, by the way.'

Doyle glanced at the geriatric rollercoaster. It looked prehistoric and appeared to have been installed with a hammer.

'I wouldn't have thought she'd be going fast enough to break through the spindles,' he said, frowning.

'I know what you mean, but the wood's pretty rotten. They'll be falling out on their own before long.'

Doyle and Sally then asked to see the deceased's room and were taken up by Tamika, who said she'd wait outside on the landing in case they had any questions.

The room was large, with a big window looking out over the front of the house. The afternoon sunbathed the room in a warm, yellow glow. There was a single bed with a strange, medieval-looking canopy above it, and hanging from this were countless crystals that reflected rainbow-coloured splashes of light into the darker corners of the room. Every inch of wall was covered in pictures that reflected the taste of the late owner. Unicorns, fairies, and angels predominated.

There was a small desk under the window. Doyle checked the drawers and found various papers, a cheque book, and other banking documents, all in folders and all neatly arranged. The deceased, it would seem, was a very methodical lady when it came to money, however whimsical she had been about everything else.

Sally started with the dresser, which was a bit too large for the room and had a parade ground of glass figurines on the top. Nestling behind the larger ones at the back were two empty vodka bottles. Inside a big, old-fashioned wardrobe, its doors covered in postcards and pictures cut out of magazines, clothes hung neatly on hangers. Tucked at the back, under some lavender sachets, she found an empty gin bottle.

Against one wall was a small kitchen table that held a kettle, a couple of mugs, and an electric ring of the sort favoured by those who like a snack at odd hours. Next to this was a small fridge.

The bathroom cabinet contained the usual remedies. Aspirin, indigestion mixture, vitamin pills. It all seemed very ordinary in a slightly 'alternative' way. The only anomalies were the spirit bottles that seemed to have been hidden, but not very well. Sally dusted them for prints and found some good ones on the necks of the bottles. She photographed them to compare with those taken from the deceased, then bagged the empties to take with her.

They closed and secured the door, then Doyle and Sally returned to the brightly coloured corpse. Tamika continued going down, the breeze made by her passing causing strands of purple hair to wave like ragged feathers.

Doyle looked around, then up and down, 'What about

those empties, Sally? Could she have been out of it and lost her footing?'

'It's possible, of course, but we'll see what the post-mortem turns up.'

'Well, I'll check her bank to see if that brings up anything, but with no witnesses, no obvious motive, and no suspects lurking about in balaclavas, it looks to me like one little old lady shuffled off her mortal coil in a drunken attempt to fly.'

'Or maybe it was just time and fate.'

'I've been trying to nail those bastards for years,' said Doyle with a grim smile.

He sought out Galadriel and asked her for Mrs Meldrum's personal details. As she burrowed frantically amongst the piles of paper on her desk, Tamika opened the filing cabinet and found what he needed. Doyle dutifully wrote down all the pertinent information, then tracked down his guvnor, who was now sitting in the dining room next to an elderly lady festooned with occult jewellery. She was holding his hand, palm up, and mumbling about lifelines. Seeing his sergeant, Franks got up quickly, took his leave with obvious relief, and followed Doyle outside.

After hearing his sergeant's report, he said, 'I want you in charge of this one. There's probably nothing in it, but we may as well have the case as that uniform lot. It'll look good on my weekly report.'

Doyle was not pleased. 'But what about Robert Smart? I can't drop that case just when I'm starting to get somewhere at last.'

'Christ, Doyle, give it a rest, will you?' replied his superior impatiently. 'Just because he's from your part of the world doesn't mean he's important. Besides, face it, he's too bloody cunning for you, mate.' Doyle stared at a spot just above Franks' left ear and said nothing, so the DI continued. 'I'll get a lift back to the nick with uniform. Call the coroner's office if those idiots haven't done it yet. And make up a case file when you get back. We'll have a 'suspicious' on for a day or two, then mark it 'accidental' and job done. Another case solved. *Solved*, got it? Not like your endless wild goose chase after Smart.'

With that, he lumbered off to commandeer a seat in Rickets' vehicle.

Sally waved as she shepherded her boss to their van and yelled that she'd send him a report in a day or two. She then drove off, leaving Doyle on his own, which was actually how he preferred it. He wanted to have a talk with the only calm, rational person he'd found in this place. What was her name? Tamika, that was it.

~~~

Sergeant Rickets viewed having to chauffeur DI Franks as a personal insult but could do bugger all about it. To vent his spleen, however, he decided to leave his idiot of a constable with Farmer's bagman. That would stop the Irish bastard stealing the silver, if nothing else. He looked around for Pugh, then remembered he had instructed him to wait at the junction of the main road to help SOCO and CID find the place. Stupid bugger must still be there. Rickets sighed and drove up the lane to where PC Pugh was indeed still standing.

Constable Pugh was of average height but extremely thin, his uniform enveloping him like a blue serge carapace with shiny buttons. The instant he saw DI Franks in the back of the car, he drew to attention and saluted.

Rickets swore (silently) in disgust, then told Pugh to go back to the house and liaise with the detective sergeant. 'When the mortuary van arrives, make sure the body gets signed for. DS Doyle will bring you back to the nick.'

Watching Rickets' car disappear down the road, PC Pugh uttered a short prayer for the safety of his sergeant, then walked up to the big house and found Doyle in the dining room talking to a very attractive dark-haired woman. The DS was polite to him (unusual, in Pugh's experience) and suggested he go have a chat with the residents in the lounge, which Pugh was very happy to do. He got on well with old folks.

When he entered the room, he found four elderly people. Two of them were dressed in what he thought was most inappropriate attire. Elderly people were supposed to wear sober colours, carry bibles, and smell of mothballs. These two looked as if they were dressed for some sort of pagan festival. The other two inhabitants looked normal, however. One was a regulation little old lady (white hair, pale pink twinset, vague smile) and the other a grey-haired gentleman reading a newspaper in a large chair by the fire. The old man looked up and spoke when Pugh entered the room.

'What the fuck do you want, copper? Piss off!'

'Now, now,' said the normal-looking lady, who was very properly knitting. 'Don't be rude to the young man, Mr Bendix. He's only doing his duty.' She gave Pugh a smile that reminded him of warm scones and stories before bedtime.

Galadriel entered the room and handed him a cup of something hot that smelt of wet blankets.

'When are you going to remove poor Mrs Meldrum?' she

asked plaintively.

'We're just waiting for the morgue to send a vehicle to collect the deceased, ma'am,' he replied sombrely. 'I'm sure this must have been very upsetting for everyone here. You have my condolences.'

He was about to broach the subject of leading them in a short prayer when the doorbell rang.

Constable Pugh followed Galadriel into the hall, where they found two men in white coats. The taller of the two introduced himself as Mr Funnel. He was the senior mortuary attendant, he said, acting on instructions from the coroner's office. He had a clipboard and clearly knew how to use it. His partner was very short and looked like an inquisitive chipmunk. He was introduced as Mr Bright.

The constable got out his pocketbook and made a careful note of both the attendants' names. This seemed to please Mr Funnel, who reciprocated by jotting something down on his clipboard.

The two men and the constable walked over to the staircase and looked up. Mrs Meldrum looked down. Her head was tilted to one side as if asking how on Earth they were going to extricate her from her predicament.

Constable Pugh could not help being impressed with the two collectors of the dead. They had the same professional manner as plumbers or electricians. They stood for a moment, hands on hips, sucking their teeth and pondering the problem. The impact had folded the old lady's body into a shape that reminded Pugh of one of those bent nail puzzles you get in Christmas crackers. With only a little unbending and upending, however, the men were able to slip the body neatly into the heavy plastic bag on the gurney. Like putting a brightly coloured crane fly into an envelope, thought Galadriel. Signatures were exchanged in pocketbook and clipboard, and Mrs Meldrum was wheeled out of the house and lifted into the back of the van. Constable Pugh stood to attention and saluted as the vehicle drove away.

Then, as Sgt Rickets had said he would, DS Doyle drove him back to Glastonbury. They didn't talk much during the journey. Each was thinking his own thoughts about the day's events.

Pugh was trying to figure out how to work the story into Bible class that evening. He was sure there must be a pertinent verse, but right now he was at a loss.

Doyle was mulling over a slight feeling of disquiet, as nebulous as a faraway scent on the breeze. But what possible motive could anyone have had for doing away with the poor old lady? Of course, he hadn't interviewed all the residents yet (Tamika had said there were several more who had been away for various reasons). But the better part of his mind was still seething about Franks' comments and the time this case would take away from doing a bit of real police work. Robert Smart was from the province all right — Doyle could almost see the bowler hat and orange sash — and was clearly up to something lucrative and probably dirty. Men like Smart never change no matter where they live. Doyle had heard that he was into loan sharking and part of the drugs network. It wasn't just his instincts that told him this man needed taking out as soon as possible to make the world a better place. And Paddy Doyle wanted very much to make the world a better place. That was why he had become a copper.

*Chapter 2*

At last the route to the upper floors was open and the residents could go to their rooms and the comfort of their own toilets. As Granny Toogood passed by the door of the late Mrs Meldrum's room, she smiled at the 'Police, DO NOT ENTER' sign. It didn't worry her. She knew she had left no fingerprints behind.

The evening meal that night was a sombre affair. Only Mrs Spottiswood and the Major joined Galadriel, and none of them were really hungry. Nothing was said of the late Mrs Meldrum as the three of them picked over the vegetable bake Tamika had left in the oven before going home. It was all too horrible for words.

Afterwards, Galadriel cleared up and washed the dishes by hand (the dishwasher was broken again), then went around checking that each 'guest' was in their room and, after the tragic events of the day, still alive. At last, when all was finally quiet, Galadriel left the house and went to what she called her 'bower'. This was an old caravan that squatted under a clump of trees at the side of the grounds, the walk to which was made interesting by broken paving stones and wet undergrowth. It had once been her private place for contemplation and crystal gazing but was now her bedroom because all the apartments in the house needed to be let. The outside was decorated with faded mystical symbols and partially hidden by overgrown bush ivy and nettles. Some of the windows were covered with thick curtains. Moss, mould, and bird droppings coated the sagging roof.

Her cat, Bast, was asleep on the steps and she would have bent down to stroke him, but he heard her coming, opened one yellow eye, and slunk off, growling. Inside were rows of books and piles of magazines on a small table. Beyond that was the construct she used as a bed, above which swathes of dark blue and purple cloth were arranged to hide the low ceiling. Tiny fairy lights had been woven into constellations and attached to the cloth. There were also lots of scented candles and joss sticks, but these had less to do with aromatherapy than the smell of damp, rot, and a fiercely male cat.

It had been one foul, horrible, bloody day. And to think she had recently been nursing hopes that Grey Havens might at last be on the up.

'On the up!' she said scathingly to her reflection in a small mirror. 'Yes, tits up!'

Things had been bad enough when Mrs Spratt had died while staying at her brother's a few months ago. Galadriel had had nightmares about not being able to find another tenant, especially since the roof above the dormer window in that room had started leaking. When it rained, Tamika and Doris were constantly up and down the stairs with buckets to keep water from going through the floor to the room below. Not that her alleged business partner, Geoff bloody Bendix, cared. He told her he'd have it fixed when she had a firm agreement with a new tenant. Well, she didn't have that yet, but Miss Browne had seemed rather nice when she came to look around the place, and hopefully she was not the type to be frightened off by an accidental death. According to Mrs Spottiswood, who'd known her for many years when she lived in London, Miss Browne was very independent, volunteered for all sorts of good causes, and was passionate about her collection of pot plants, which apparently she made a habit of talking to. Galadriel thought this all sounded promising. Even better, she had offered to pay six months' rent in advance. But now there would be another empty room and where the hell was she going to find someone to plug that financial gap?

Galadriel readied herself for bed, which involved a quick wash in the tiny bathroom and a flannelette nighty to keep out the chill. She was beyond tired, but her brain would not shut off. Money. There was never enough of it, never. She'd call that bastard Geoff in the morning. As she lay and wished for oblivion, her mind raced over lovers that had left, plans that had unravelled, and hopes that had been dashed, but always circled back to Geoff Bendix.

He had eased his way into her life some three years before. He had made no pretence of being a gentleman, but presented himself as an entrepreneur, a man of business. In fact, he was a conman, but one who, once he had a scam up and running, believed in it with all the fervour of a religious convert.

He owned a few properties around the town. They were the sort that were always on the verge of being condemned and formed the last refuge of the down-but-not-quite-out. He owned a building company, too, which enabled him to play merry hell with the VAT and save a fortune when it came to bodging repairs on his born-again slums. He also owned a scrapyard that was near enough to Galadriel's property for her to smell the burning tyres. This enterprise was not the gold mine it had once been, but it still made a few quid and came in handy at odd times. Geoff was always willing to 'educate a shilling,' as he put it, and sometimes invested in little schemes presented to him by his fellow bottom feeders in the river of commerce. He was well known to them as a man so twisted he could swallow a nail and shit a corkscrew.

Grey Havens Retirement Apartments had, in fact, been his idea and, for him, it was a surprisingly good one. Its impetus had been his desire to winkle his old father out of his ex-council house in Stepney so he could rent it for a good price and then sell it when the bugger died, which he fervently hoped would be soon. His arrangement with Galadriel was very simple: he ran the 'boring' financial side of things while she managed the house. A division of labour that had seemed like a blessing to Galadriel, until it became a curse.

She felt no better the next morning, having slept little and badly, but the smell of breakfast being prepared by Tamika gave the day an almost normal start, as if yesterday had happened to someone else. Tamika was subdued, however, and young Doris slumped red-eyed at the kitchen table, chewing toast. She was a local girl, well-meaning if not very bright, and incredibly superstitious. Folklore and country adages, she'd learned at the feet of her granny ruled her life. On the table surrounding her plate were a rabbit's foot, strange roots tied with ribbon, and a horseshoe. She was refusing to vacuum the stairs.

'Until the place be shriven, I daren't set foot on the cursed spot!' she wailed.

Tamika kindly told her to go clean the utility room instead

and she would see what could be done.

After a quick breakfast, Galadriel walked through the hall, her eyes drawn involuntarily to the gap in the stair rails, and into her office. She closed the door and lit a candle. A candle that was full of rare, potent ingredients, guaranteed to release healing essences into the air. At the moment, all she asked of it was to mask the smell of a very common and wholly detrimental cigarette. She lit up, inhaled deeply, and called Geoff.

As she'd expected, the phone rang until the answer machine kicked in. She listened to the voice of Geoff's 'secretary', Tina, a young blonde whose talents were undoubtedly more physical than mental.

'Bendix Holdings, no one is in the office at the moment, but if you'd like to leave your name and number, we will call you back as soon as possible.'

'Geoff, it's me' Galadriel said. 'Get your sorry arse over here as soon as possible. There has been a death and the police are all over the place.'

That should do it, she thought, slamming down the phone. The bastard would have to emerge from hiding now, despite the broken washing machine and dryer, which, she was sure, was the reason she had not seen hide nor hair of him for two weeks.

She sat at her desk and scowled at the piles of paper, ethnic ornaments, and mugs full of innumerable pens and pencils. There was also an assortment of deities of various denominations, including a small Buddha she'd had since her first ever Glastonbury Festival. The headliners had been David Bowie, Joan Baez, Fairport Convention, and Quintessence that year. The music of her past. But now, to a fifty-year-old

Galadriel, the past was not only another country, it was a
completely different planet.

For a start, her birth certificate declared her to be Doreen
Mudd, born in Peckham in 1946. Hers had been a sheltered
childhood and her parents did not hold with any of this
'teenage' nonsense. She had worked in a shop, dressed just like
her mother, and allowed only a hint of makeup or boyfriends.
But she had left that name behind, together with her virginity
when she had escaped and went to that first Glastonbury in
1971. And she'd been here ever since, more or less. Apart from
a quick trip to India in the curry-stained clutches of the guru
Shangravista, anyway. He had given her a mantra, his celestial
blessing, and thrush. Of these, the thrush had lasted longest.

So, she had become Galadriel Starchild of the tribe of
Hippie, and over the years had tried most things to make ends
meet. Or, if not meet, then come as close together as possible.
Thanks to the concerts and the whole New Age movement,
Glastonbury had become a place where you could get a karmic
massage or a vaginal smoke douche easier than a tin of baked
beans. Shops specialized in mystic paraphernalia and occult
jewellery, soothsayers and sages advertised on crudely painted
signs that blocked the pavement, and beautiful people skipped
barefoot to the tunes of street musicians. Galadriel knew her
way around the avenues of expanded consciousness, and a few
cul-de-sacs as well. She had opened a shop with a young man
who would only sell his wares to people whose cosmic aura was
in harmony with his handmade dream catchers. He caught the
dreams; she caught a financial cold because it was her name on
the rent book. After that she waited at tables in some of the
small cafés that proliferated. Their names might change pretty

frequently, 'Faery's Grotto' becoming 'Anwyn's Urn' overnight, but the brownies remained the same.

Then fate finally lent a hand in the form of an elderly lady whom Galadriel had befriended and cared for in her final illness. Upon her death, Galadriel was astonished to find she had been left the woman's entire property. She was thrilled to become the owner of a big house with lots of rooms, even if it did have a leaky roof and antediluvian plumbing. Galadriel took possession and, at the advice of her friend Millie, opened the place as a guest house during festival season. Word got around, friends told friends, and before she knew it the place was heaving with brightly clothed individuals mingling together in a haze of pot smoke and patchouli oil. All very well, but no one paid, and she still had to clean up afterwards. Positive vibes and serene energies are fine, but they don't unblock the sink or buy lavatory paper.

Millie was one of the many who stayed on for months, not quite squatting because she did pay Galadriel now and then and sometimes helped about the place. Recognizing a good thing when she had it, Millie then suggested a year-round guest house with a New Age slant. She even put a bit of money into redecorating. Galadriel put herself into hock and bought proper beds and new bedding, had the roof in the summer house fixed and called it the 'Ashram'. And thus, Rainbow Lodge was born. She might have made a go of it, too, except for a certain Mr Dereck Billings, otherwise known as Dr Bleat. He was a musician famous for re-treading his old pop hits and screwing his young groupies. The younger the better. His manager had tried to keep temptation away by taking a room for him at Rainbow Lodge, which was a taxi ride away from his current venue. Quite how a fifteen-year-old managed to find her way there was never established, but the News of the World had a front-page spread about it. Lights, camera, action, and a visit from the police. This was followed by nasty brown envelopes containing demands with menaces from the local council and planning department. Galadriel was well and truly stuffed. She had no money and no prospects, and it looked like she would have to sell up, in which case she would have no home, either. No bank would help her, and Millie promptly buggered off to North Wales to find herself. Galadriel clung on by her long, purple fingernails until all she had left to sell was her beloved but clapped out Morris Minor.

So, she had driven through the rusty iron gates of the scrapyard near her home. A large, surly man in grease-stained overalls told her the owner wasn't there, but if she wanted to leave the car, someone would call her with a price. At a loss, Galadriel was about to drive away when a shiny Mercedes purred into the yard and parked next to her. Out got a man she knew by sight but not by name.

Like blood in the water, news of Galadriel's financial misfortune had spread in the sea of Glastonbury gossip. Enter Geoff Bendix, grinning like a great white shark. He knew who she was, where she lived, and all of her circumstances. As a bolt of lightning had been sent down from some capitalist heaven, an idea burned its way through his head straight into his wallet.

When Galadriel asked him how much her car would fetch, he replied without hesitation, 'Oh, these are highly collectible just now and yours is a little gem. Will you take five hundred?'

Galadriel, who had expected a fraction of that sum, nodded

her thanks and fought back tears as she reached into the car and took out a bundle of papers, including the logbook, and handed them to Geoff. He patted her on the shoulder and went into the garage, emerging a moment later with a bundle of used notes. He thrust these into her hand and asked if she would like a lift home.

'Do you live far?' he asked, knowing very well she didn't.

Galadriel pointed to the rooftop peeking over the trees nearby and said she would walk, then thanked him warmly and with a wan smile turned and left.

When she was gone, Geoff's foreman, Lionel, came over, kicked the offside wheel of the Morris, and said 'A bit old for your taste, isn't she? The bird, I mean, not this heap of shit.'

'Mind your own fucking business. And while you're doing it, put a new set of tyres on this heap. Well, ones with more tread than these, anyway. Then steam clean the engine, replace the plugs, make sure the brakes are all right, and give it a good polish. Then take it over to Bent Bernie and get a new MOT.'

Geoff withdrew to the oily recesses of a huge brick garage and workshop. At the back was a partitioned space he used as an office. After switching on the light, he sat in his big swivel chair, reached into the desk, and took out a bottle of cheap whisky. Then, lighting a cigar and putting his feet up on a decrepit sofa, he savoured the brilliant idea that had come to him with such clarity only a moment ago. As soon as he had seen Galadriel, he knew she was the key to the best scheme he'd ever hatched. A middle-aged hippy with no money but one big asset: a huge house that could easily and cheaply be turned into small apartments for the elderly, starting with his own aged and crabby father. The old bastard was sitting on a fortune; what had once been a huge council housing estate in East London was now on the verge of becoming trendy. The home his father had bought for just over four thousand pounds as a sitting tenant was now worth three times that at least. Rentals in London so near the City were fetching big bucks. All he had to do was park the old sod on Galadriel and the rest would be easy. Geoff sat in his smoke-filled cubbyhole and dreamed a dream. One that would enrich him for years to come and hopefully see off his bloody father sooner rather than later.

A few days after their first meeting, therefore, Geoff drove up to Rainbow Lodge in Galadriel's Morris Minor. It was much cleaner and in far better repair now, and the paintwork had been touched up (as had the MOT certificate). Geoff got out and, holding a bundle of wildflowers wrapped in ferns, stood looking up at the huge, forbidding edifice. He could see at once there were some serious issues with it. He was a builder, after all. Not a very good one, but he'd knocked about the industry long enough to pick up some basic knowledge of old buildings. This one towered over him. Three floors plus what was probably servants' quarters in the attic. The roof was slate, and two tall chimney stacks could be seen from this side. There would be more, and they were always a nightmare to repair. On his left, a large bay window curved around. That would be a reception room. An arched doorway under a carved stone cornice looked like the entrance to a church or a mausoleum. On his right was another big, wide window of dressed stone with leaded panes at the top. A bugger to repair and they invariably leaked or let in a draft.

He walked up the steps and banged with the huge brass doorknocker. Galadriel opened the door, her mass of orange-red hair trailing down overflowing cheesecloth garments and a market stall's worth of ethnic jewellery. She was surprised to see him. She was even more surprised to see her old Morris parked in the drive behind him. But, on second glance, she realized it wasn't her 'old' Morris. This was a 'new' old Morris. It looked so beautiful it took her breath away. Geoff put the car keys (now on a fob bearing the logo of Bendix Holdings) into her hand and told her the car was hers once again. New MOT, new tyres, the lot. Then he handed her the flowers, which were, of course, perfect.

Galadriel was completely overwhelmed, but eventually pulled herself together enough to invite him inside.

'The thing is,' he said as they sat in her big kitchen, 'I'm a great believer in doing what I can to help souls in trouble.' He took her hand across the table. 'I know you are having problems, and I know what it's like when officialdom prevents you from living the life you were meant to live.'

'All I want to do' said Galadriel looking at him earnestly, 'is use this lovely old house to make the world a better place.'

He smiled. 'Show me around' he said. 'Being a master builder, I'm interested in this extraordinary home of yours.'

The charm was laid on thick as treacle while Galadriel took him over the entire house. He made appreciative noises, but they were always followed by some worrying caveat regarding the condition of the building. Actually, it wasn't as bad as he thought it would be. Until, that is, they got to the attic rooms and he could see daylight through some of the ceilings.

They returned to the kitchen and, over some ghastly hot beverage Galadriel called tea, he encouraged her to tell him the story of her life. There was nothing in it that caused him any surprise. It all seemed quite normal to him, for Glastonbury, anyway.

Eventually, he looked at his slim gold watch. 'I'm enjoying our chat immensely,' he said, 'but I'm afraid I have to get back to work now. I'd like to help you, though, Galadriel. Shall we have dinner together soon? There's a new vegetarian restaurant just opened nearby that I'm told is quite good.'

'I'd really like that,' she said. 'And thank you for giving me my car back. And for listening to me.'

The following week, Geoff took her to a small restaurant out of town. He had chosen the venue carefully and Galadriel was duly impressed. It had been a long time since she had been taken anywhere nice for a meal, and never had she been wined and dined by a player as smooth as Geoff when he was planning a coup. Cocktails were followed by wine with the meal. Then, over coffee and fine brandy, he made his opening salvo.

From his briefcase he took a handful of brochures from private retirement homes, and pad of paper. With a few strokes of his gold pen he mapped out his vision for Grey Havens Retirement Apartments. Galadriel sat enthralled as the candlelight illuminated plans for a comfortable and worry-free future.

'You have a wonderful house, but time has taken its toll and the decay that threatens it must be stopped. Dry rot, wet rot, crumbling masonry, a leaking roof; but with my help we can turn the place into a home again. A warm, comfortable home that is also a spiritual hub, a true haven.' Geoff had done his homework well.

He drew a plan of each floor of the house and explained how, with certain alterations, bedrooms could become apartments.

Self-contained apartments that could be let for proper money. More brandy was poured and, as Galadriel's glass was filled with amber liquid, so her mind was filled with visions of her house born again as a caring sanctuary for the elderly.

'People like my dear old dad,' said Geoff, 'who want more than just a lonely room in which to spend their twilight days. There will be no shortage of people who will gratefully gravitate to this harmonious, spiritual Wessex home. And of course, my connections in the local council and masonic lodge will ensure there are no planning problems or delays.'

With a few simple sums he showed her how, with a little investment (provided by himself) and using local artisans (courtesy of Bendix Enterprises) her house would live anew in harmony with the infinite and have working drains. But as a money-making venture, albeit one with a soul.

He was at his best that evening. A master of his craft spinning wonderful dreams and visions. No gaudy fly ever walked into a web of deceit more naively than Galadriel.

He drove her home through tiny lanes that seemed more like green tunnels. In the stark headlights, Geoff thought the place looked as forbidding as a prison or an asylum. But what Galadriel saw was that 'last homely house' as described by her favourite author. She saw a haven where those of like mind could spend their retirement years.

Geoff left her with a chaste farewell, not even a peck on the cheek, and drove the short distance to his scrapyard. He parked, lit a cigar, and contemplated Galadriel's roof against the night sky. It would be a bloody huge job, but it was doable. And if it worked, he would have a new business to plunder. If didn't, oh well, it was Galadriel who would take the fall.

He threw his cigar stub out the window and drove home.

Geoff's solicitor drew up an agreement that Galadriel signed after looking at it with some concern. It was awfully long, she said.

'Don't you worry your head about that, my dear,' he reassured her. 'Legal documents always look unfriendly, don't they? But we have to make sure you are protected and of course I'll change anything you don't like. I just need something to show the bank to cover my investment.'

In the end, Galadriel didn't even get a copy, but while the sun was shining and the builders worked their magic, it didn't seem to matter much.

Of course, nothing ever goes exactly to plan, and Geoff found the house was not as amenable to reconstruction as he'd hoped. It was only because he had the building inspector in his pocket that he got away with as much as he did.

The only thing Galadriel insisted on was handling the recruitment of staff. Geoff had envisioned some nice, easily frightened young illegals from the fringes of the agricultural sector. There were always fruit pickers looking for less arduous jobs out of the mud and bullying, and they would be cheap.

Galadriel was having none of that. For a start, she wanted an administrator of some kind. Someone to handle paperwork and telephone calls. And a chef, of course. Then a cleaner, someone local and trustworthy. She also wanted a healer/masseur who could administer to the holistic needs of the residents.

This last demand caused Geoff to put his foot down in a way that should have warned Galadriel of things to come. There was, he told her, a whole town full of healers and massage merchants under a mile away. The residents could get a fucking bus.

In the end, the only staff she got that met her actual specifications was Doris, who was indeed trustworthy and came from a local family that had supplied servants to all the big houses in the area for generations.

The administrator and the chef came in the form of one young woman named Tamika Jones, a single parent in her early thirties who had a degree in business studies and a Jamaican auntie who had taught her how to cook. But, because Tamika lived out, Galadriel still had to perform some of the catering duties herself.

Getting residents, though, was even easier than Geoff had said it would be. Galadriel made discreet enquiries and put cards up in the right sort of places. These resulted in Mrs Spottiswood and Mrs Meldrum, who knew Mrs Spratt, who knew Mr Tiptree. The *Fortean Times* netted Miss Langdolin, and she brought her sister Mrs Prout-Smythe with her. Geoff only ended up providing two residents. One of these was Mrs Toogood, a lady his Masonic chum had met at a funeral; the other was his father, Bert.

Bert Bendix was down with pneumonia at the time and was hardly aware of his move from a small, scruffy council house to Grey Havens. His room was one of the best: first floor front with a big bathroom and a sitting room that had a view of the Tor. Geoff paid no rent for this, of course, because, as he explained, he had to recover all of his building costs first.

Within a few months all the apartments had been taken and the residents were paying rent to Bendix Holdings, which skimmed a hefty chunk off the top for repayments and disbursements. What was left got paid into Galadriel's bank account, but it was never much. In the early days, Geoff would pop in regularly to see how things were going, but now he stayed away as much as possible. When it came right down to it, the only regular thing in Geoff Bendix's life was his gambling, and that was well and truly out of control.

*Chapter 3*

Geoff didn't get Galadriel's message until about six that evening when he wandered into the office to see if there was any money in the petty cash box. His first thought was that it was some sort of joke. His second thought was that, if it wasn't a joke, then it probably had something to do with his father. The old bastard was certainly capable of violence. Then he had a third thought: if the police were there then he didn't want to be, regardless of the reason.

In the end, he decided to drive to his scrapyard and scout out the area on the way. If there were ambulances or police cars at Galadriel's place, he would take a little holiday and say he never got the message. Before leaving, he wiped the tape and unplugged the answering machine, just in case.

He saw nothing that hinted at trouble on his way to the yard, but even so he decided to park there and walk through the woods to Grey Havens so he could suss out the situation without being seen. There was nothing at the front of the house to denote any catastrophe. He crept around the side, ducking under the windows. Nothing untoward that he could see in the lounge. No body on the floor, anyway. The next room in line was Galadriel's office. He furtively peeked through the open curtains. No, there was nothing there either.

He went around the back of the house and, skirting the shrubbery, crept towards the open back door to the kitchen. He could hear the sound of voices and the clatter of crockery. As he got closer, the appetising smell of a curry made him realize how hungry he was. A day passed in the bookmakers gave one an appetite. He peeked around the door. There was Tamika, stirring a large pot on the stove. It all seemed very normal.

Stepping through the doorway, he said 'So, what the fuck is going on? Who's dead and what's all this about the ruddy police?'

Tamika ignored him and carried on stirring. No curry for him, then.

'Keep your bloody voice down' said Galadriel. She sounded angry. He was rather glad when she put down the knife she was using to chop vegetables.

She quickly dried her hands and then led him to her office. As they passed through the utility room, he saw a sign saying, 'Fucking Bust Again!!!' stuck to the dishwasher. He pretended not to notice.

Once in the office, Galadriel shut the door with a lot more force than it needed, sat down at her desk, and reached for a packet of cigarettes. She didn't offer him one.

'That stairlift you fitted has probably killed one of the tenants' she said as she lit up.

'Do what? You stoned?'

'Poor Mrs Meldrum has had a fall. Well, more than a fall actually. She's passed over.'

'Passed over what?'

'Passed over to the other side, Geoff! The poor woman is

dead, and the police have been here and — '

Geoff interrupted her. 'Was my father involved? Did he push her? Have the Old Bill got him or what?'

'No, of course not, he wasn't even in the house at the time. It was an accident. At least, they haven't said it wasn't and I can't imagine how it could be. Anyway, she hit your rotten stairlift that's been stuck halfway up for weeks.'

Geoff could see that the hand holding the cigarette was trembling and he knew he would get nowhere by leading off so he sat down and as calmly and smoothly as he could pitch it, asked her to tell him all about it. She told him.

His overall reaction was one of relief. Old people fell down stairs all the time. It was a shame his father was neither the victim nor the culprit, but you couldn't have everything.

Leaving Galadriel to smoke another cigarette and recover a bit, he went out into the hall. Through the open door of the lounge he saw a little old lady in a wing chair by the front window. She was knitting and didn't seem to notice him. (Except, of course, she did. Granny Toogood missed nothing. From where she sat could see who came to the house and, with the doors open in this warm weather, hear a lot as well. She was content. Apparently, there had been no mention of foul play by the police. Early days, but even so, she felt reasonably safe. She knitted on, the click and clack of her needles sounding like bones rattling.)

Geoff examined the stairlift. He'd only installed the thing to placate his father. The old man had moaned that he couldn't manage the stairs and was threatening to move back to his own house. Not that he could have done, because by then Geoff had let it out and was getting a damn good rent for it, too. It had been a stroke of luck that this bit of equipment had been brought to the yard for scrap. He'd get his apprentice, Desmond, to come over and sort it, along with the broken balustrades.

Should he visit his father? Well, why not, he was nearly there anyway. Outside his father's room, he could hear the television quite clearly through the mahogany door. He banged as loudly as he could without breaking a knuckle. The sound diminished and a voice that sounded like a drain cover being dragged across concrete, shouted 'Who's there?'

'It's Geoff, Dad. Your son, Geoff.'

A slight pause, then, 'Fuck off!' and the sound of the television being turned up louder than before.

No change there then, he thought, and wished again that it had been his father's bull neck that had been broken on the stairs.

Geoff stuck his head around the door to Galadriel's office and told her he would send someone around tomorrow to fix the stairlift and the balustrades. Then he was off like a shot before he could be asked to deal with any of the other needed repairs.

A trying evening, he thought, on the drive home. He'd have to call his insurance broker and see if he could make a claim against the old biddy's estate for damage to his property. Then he remembered he hadn't actually paid the insurance premium for a month or two. Oh well, he had a hot tip on a horse running at Newmarket on Saturday. When that came in at twenty to one he'd be well in funds, so no worries.

The news of a death at Grey Havens bounced around the town, gathering momentum as it went. Mrs Meldrum had been a regular at several cafés, and a member of three spiritual circles, each of whom was claiming to have come first in the race to contact her spirit. Mr Tiptree, returning from a visit to his sister on Friday morning, was accosted by a family friend at Dandy and Lion's, a chic little watering hole in the town. Not having called in to Grey Havens first, he knew nothing of the tragedy. Therefore, when asked for details of 'the poor soul's passing,' he assumed the lady was enquiring about his sister's pampered pet, an ancient pug named Winnie who, during his recent visit, had gorged itself on the contents of next door's waste bins for the umpteenth and, as it turned out, final time.

So, he replied that the 'poor soul' had indeed passed. In fact, she had passed everything she had eaten in the previous forty-eight hours in one huge stream of effluent right there on the living room carpet.

'My dear,' he said shuddering, 'so much poo from such a small body! And then her heart gave out. But she was always rooting around in the waste bins, so it's really no wonder when you come to think of it.'

His listener was silent as she contemplated this terrible end of such a genteel-looking lady and one she had always thought to be so fastidious in her habits.

~~~

There was definitely a pall hanging over Grey Havens that had nothing to do with the various joss sticks Mrs Spottiswood was burning.

'I had better ask the Coven of the Sacred Thorn to come round,' she told Galadriel. This was a group of ladies dedicated to the ways of Wicca who met in the home of Mrs Chantry (AKA Sister Aiyana), who ran a corset and medical appliance shop. Sister Aiyana was a large, muscular lady with a moustache who knew her way around the pagan mysteries better than anyone Mrs Spottiswood had yet come across.

Galadriel thanked her but said that, just at the moment, with the stairs in the condition they were in and the police tape still across poor Mrs Meldrum's door, it might all be a bit too much.

Tamika said, 'Someone is going to have to contact Mrs Meldrum's sister and arrange for her belongings to be collected.'

That was enough for Galadriel. 'Oh, yes, please do, Tamika,' she said, then fled to her office where, after rooting around in the petty cash tin, she left a note saying she needed to go into town for some things.

~~~

Tamika was in the kitchen washing up after lunch when Geoff's apprentice, Desmond, came in. He was called an 'apprentice' because that enabled Geoff to get a government grant and save a bit of money on what were already meagre wages. Desmond was in his late twenties and had a degree in archaeology as well as the longest dreadlocks Tamika had ever seen. He could also fix just about anything electrical or mechanical.

Desmond grabbed a towel and started drying the dishes. As they got through the piles of crockery, Tamika told him about Mrs Meldrum, the police, and all the rest. They had coffee, then went to inspect the damage. Desmond said it was all fixable.

'I'll have the stairlift working in no time,' he said. 'Then I'll replace the balustrades. They won't be turned mahogany like the originals, of course. Geoff said to get some broom handles and cut them to size.'

Typical, thought Tamika. Leaving Desmond to get on with it, she went upstairs to see Bert. She knocked a code on the door so he would know it was her and refrain from his usual obscene response to visitors.

Bert Bendix was eighty-three, bad-tempered, foul-mouthed, and anti-social. He had once been a professional boxer, amongst other things, and still radiated barely suppressed rage when provoked. He was short and stocky, with closely cropped grey hair and features that bore witness to his interesting and violent past. From the day of his arrival, the only person who could cope with him was Tamika. She had taken no notice when he led off, swearing and cursing in his East London slang. Even when he made racist remarks that caused everyone else to shudder, she just smiled and called him an old gangster who should have been hanged years ago.

Bert had hated the move to Grey Havens. He knew it had come about just so his arse of a son could let out his house, and the fact that he had been too sick to prevent it made him hate it all the more. Geoff said the rent money was going to pay for his new apartment and provide an addition to his old age pension, but Bert knew his son better than that.

Initially, his biggest moan had been about the food. 'It's all bloody vegetables and these fucking bean things! I've fed me rabbits better stuff than this!' he had roared when Galadriel tried to introduce him to a healthy vegetarian diet.

Bert took to paying Doris to go into town on her bike and get him fish and chips, but Tamika eventually solved the problem by enlisting her Auntie Grace to cook for him.

Tamika's mother and aunt had come from Jamaica on the *Windrush* and settled in Bristol. Tamika's mother had died soon after giving birth to her, so Auntie Grace, one of the best cooks who ever ran a works canteen, had raised her. (Tamika never knew who her father was, but her aunt's views on the British Navy made her suspect he had been a sailor.) Auntie Grace was now retired and a pillar of her local church, but for the cost of ingredients only, she would cook Bert the kind of meals he loved. Sometimes Tamika heated them up for him in the kitchen, but mostly he just microwaved them in his room. And every other Sunday Bert would be helped down the stairs, into Tamika's car, and driven off to Auntie's for a proper Sunday lunch. She even had bottled beer chilled and ready for him. It wasn't long before Bert became part of the family. The rude part. He enjoyed playing with Tamika's seven-year-old daughter, Daisy. Daisy's father, like Tamika's, had not been involved much beyond conception, so Bert revelled in being the only male. As a result, he was perfectly happy at Grey Havens now, but would rather be burned at the stake than admit this to his rotten, no-good, useless son.

Tamika went in, put the kettle on for a cup of tea, and updated Bert on the situation. He rarely went down to the communal room. As far as he was concerned, the other residents were bloody loonies. He enjoyed annoying Mrs Spottiswood whose apartment was on the same landing as his and who was always complaining about how loud his television was. Tamika had got him a set of headphones, but he mostly 'forgot' to use them.

After tea, she went back downstairs and found Desmond in the utility room with the innards of the dishwasher strewn all over the floor. She sat down on a discarded kitchen chair to keep him company.

'Bendix is a tight bastard' he said, rummaging around in the rubber pipes. 'These things are cheap enough to buy, but he just won't.'

'I don't think he's actually got much money,' said Tamika. 'Bills are always being paid late. The phone was even cut off for a few days last month.' She passed him a spanner. 'I hope he at least fixes the roof. A friend of Mrs Spottiswood's wants to move into the top floor and another rent would really help.'

'Might change her mind after Wednesday's little accident. Not good for trade, having a death like that in the place.' Desmond emerged from the dishwasher with a broken rubber pipe in his hands. 'Fancy a drink over the weekend?'

Tamika smiled. 'No,' she said, 'but thank you for sorting out that machine. Come into the kitchen when you've finished, and I'll make you a sandwich.'

A Glastonbury Tale

*Chapter 4*

Saturday morning was sunny and warm. Geoff Bendix was looking forward to Newmarket as he sat in the small dining room of his nondescript house on an unremarkable housing estate six miles out of town. More importantly, he was feeling lucky. One of his credit cards still had some money on it, and his payment to Mr Smart wasn't due until the following week. While Smart's loans were handshake deals, Geoff was well aware that if the loan was not repaid on time, the hand was forfeited. So, he would definitely have to pay up, but not today. And for Geoff, today was all that mattered.

The residents of Grey Havens were also feeling better. After all, they were of an age where they had seen a death or two. Major Dennis and Granny Toogood had seen (and caused) more than a few, in fact, though in the Major's case they were carried out in the service of his Queen, who was so grateful she had given him a medal.

Somerset, once known as 'The Summer Land' is bosky and fertile. Grey Havens had been built between a couple of ancient trackways that were now tarmacked lanes. These came together at the foot of the Tor, which rose high above the surrounding countryside. From the house you could cross the lane, walk through a field, then an orchard, and up a steep path that led to the ruined tower on the summit. This iconic, and some would say (if they were not out of breath), mystical place gave you a view over three counties and Wales.

The grounds of Grey Havens sloped gently down to the house and were as verdant as the rest of Somerset. There had once been extensive lawns, including one for croquet, a tennis court, and a vegetable garden with a greenhouse and a large orchard. Now large trees dotted the site and the open space upon which the summer house sat was girded on all sides by thick, tall, unkempt hedges. Flowerbeds flowed over the narrow stone paths that dissected the tall grass. Galadriel loved the idea of a garden but lacked the money, expertise, and ambition to maintain one. The residents were content as long as there was easy access to the summer house. The path from the back door was getting very overgrown, however, and on Saturday morning Mrs Spottiswood complained.

'We don't want any more accidents, now do we?' she said.

So, after breakfast Galadriel drove to a nearby garden centre. She was trying to decide if a one-litre bottle of weed killer would do the job or if she'd have to pay for a five-litre one when she heard a familiar voice.

'Nasty stuff, that. Turn your garden into Mordor, it will.'

She turned and saw a bear of a man wearing a large, broad-brimmed leather hat with a long pheasant feather stuck in it. Both the man and the hat had seen better days.

'Oh, hello, Dai.'

'Fancy a cuppa?'

'Yes, sure, thanks.'

Galadriel had known Dai Griffiths for years. He was a fixture in the town, advertised himself as a mystic, and organised specialist tours for those seeking the history and magic of Glastonbury.

'Bit of a bugger that old dear falling down your stairs, wasn't it?' he asked when they were seated in the cafe. 'How you coping?'

As she told him all that had happened, he nodded and made sympathetic noises.

'I'll add Mrs Meldrum to our prayers and supplications this evening,' he said.

Dai was Chief Druid of the Ancient and Venerable Llandgrogg and he and his fellow Druids met at the Dog and Partridge on Saturday nights. After closing, they used the pub garden for their ceremonies. Tradition had it that his small soggy spot in the centre of town, was at the junction of at least four Ley Lines. At least that was what Dai told his flock. The landlord didn't mind so long as they kept the noise down. Dai liked the arrangement because he would 'allow' carefully chosen tour customers to attend, which meant he almost never had to buy a drink.

'Mind you, it's an ill wind and all that' he added, passing her a cupcake.

'What do you mean?'

'The thing is, you've got another empty room, right? And I've got more people wanting to join my tours than I can find housing for. We have a website now, you know, and lots of people want to do Glastonbury. From all over the world! Australia, America, you name it. Even without a festival this year.'

The Glastonbury Festival had been running for twenty-five years and was a fixture both in the landscape and on the international music scene. Officially, Glastonbury was a small market town of about 8000 inhabitants. When there was a festival, though, the population was more like 80,000, most of whom paid £65 for a ticket and £5 for a programme. The town heaved with visitors, young and old, rich and poor, sane and otherwise. The festival in 1995 had been especially huge so a decision had been made to skip a year to allow the land and the organizers to recover. This pleased the people responsible for cleaning the streets and unblocking the public conveniences, but not the shopkeepers and pub owners.

'I'm overbooked for Mabon at the end of the month and I've had loads of enquiries for Samhain, Yule, Imbolc, Ostara, and Beltane next year,' said Dai.

Most people without a pagan calendar to hand would have been mystified, but to Galadriel, as to most of the residents of Glastonbury, these holidays were as familiar as Christmas and Easter.

'You mean you want me to keep the room open for your tour people to stay in? Gosh, I don't know, Dai. I tried that kind of thing with Rainbow Lodge and it just didn't work out. I need a full-time tenant who'll pay regular rent.'

Dai looked at her with big, soulful brown eyes, but changed the subject. He knew how to handle people like Galadriel.

'I'm sorry, I shouldn't have asked. Wrong time and all that. What did you want that weed killer for, anyway?'

'My garden is so overgrown the paths are becoming dangerous. The last thing I need is someone else falling over. That stuff was on sale, so I thought I'd give it a try.'

'No, no, you'll kill everything with that, and it's not good for the birds and the bees. The old ways are best. Do you have a scythe? No? That's probably just as well, actually, as they're a bugger to use if you don't know what you're doing. We've got one we use in the Ceremony of the Corn God; got an edge on it you wouldn't believe.' He laughed. 'Last time we performed it Brother Blannwed cut his toe off right in the middle of the service! People thought it was part of the ritual until he fainted. Still, we found the toe eventually. Sadly, it was too late to sew it back on, though. Anyway, tell you what. I'll come over tomorrow, give the place a haircut, and bring the right sort of stuff for your paths. How would that be?'

Galadriel thanked him profusely and they set a time for noon. Dai said no more about a room for his tourists at Grey Havens, but he felt confident he could talk her around in the end.

~~~

On Sunday, Dai brought wine, cheese, and a freshly baked loaf of gritty wholegrain bread with him. He thought a picnic would be bound to appeal to Galadriel, especially with him all rustic and romantic in waistcoat and shirt sleeves, wielding a scythe. She met him at the door and took him through to the garden. It was much bigger than he'd imagined. Heavily overgrown and neglected, but it felt somehow full of secrets, or at least secret places.

Galadriel took him on a tour and they ended up in a far corner of the grounds where, amid a clump of ash trees and hawthorns, the remains of two low walls could just be seen under a blanket of green-grey moss. Large, well-worked stones peeked out. Dai thought they looked similar to those in the abbey walls in town. Nearby, and nearly obscured by masses of ivy, was a circle of stones about four feet in diameter. It was topped with sheets of rusted corrugated iron held down with more stones and ringed by fierce brambles. To one who was a practicing druid and really did believe in the Green God (up to a point, anyway; certainly, after a cider or three) this hidden structure had magical (and therefore monetary) potential.

'What is it?' he asked, in hushed tones.

'It's just an old well. I had it covered up years ago to keep animals from falling in. It looked quite deep.'

Dai said nothing more. His instinct was telling him there was something here it would be worth his while to find out about, but discreetly. They moved off to where Galadriel had decided he could make a start on reclaiming the garden.

Scything is an art. It requires rhythm, balance, and strength. It also requires the scythe to be sharpened every five or ten minutes, very carefully, with a whetstone. Dai began sweeping away on what had once been a tennis court, and, all things considered, was not doing a bad job. Galadriel reclined on a blanket and watched him, drinking the wine, and feeling like someone in a Pre-Raphaelite painting.

Back in the house, Tamika had stopped by with Bert's lunch and was just about to leave again when the front doorbell rang. Oh shit, she thought. Galadriel's somewhere in the garden with ruddy Dai Griffiths doing his 'far from the madding crowd' stuff and I'll get stuck with whoever it is. No one they knew well ever came in by the front door.

It was DS Doyle.

'Don't you coppers ever have a day off?' she asked, letting him in. Tamika didn't particularly like or trust the police.

'Sometimes, but I thought you'd want to get back to normal

as soon as possible. I just have a few more questions before you can have your room back.'

That seemed fair enough. Tamika was going to take him through to the office when, to her surprise, she heard herself offering him coffee. He was surprised, too, but said 'Yes, please', so she led him through to the kitchen. As she stood grinding the beans and laying out all the appropriate paraphernalia, Doyle sat at the kitchen table and looked around the big room. Amongst other things, it contained an ancient range and a huge Welsh Dresser festooned with plates, jugs, vintage crockery, and an assortment of ornaments. It was a comfortable room, old-fashioned and homely. In fact, despite its size, it reminded him of his grandmother's cottage in County Fermanagh. But that was at least one lifetime ago and he forced his mind away from the memories.

He and Tamika were just about to drink their coffee when someone screamed.

'It's coming from the garden,' said Tamika, and rushed outside, followed by Doyle.

Galadriel emerged from the orchard at a run. 'Get a towel, anything! Dai's had a terrible accident!'

Tamika ran into the kitchen and came back with a bundle of clean tea towels and a first aid kit. They followed Galadriel and found Dai holding one hand in the other and dripping alarming quantities blood onto the grass. Doyle determine it was a bad cut near the base of the thumb. He wrapped a towel around the wound and told Dai to hold his hand above his head. Unfortunately, the first aid kit Tamika had brought leaned heavily towards the alternative rather than the practical. Aloe vera, tea tree oil, and witch hazel no doubt have their uses, but it was bandages Doyle was after.

He helped Dai back to the house, then went to his car and got his own first aid kit. Dai's hand was soon clean and bandaged.

'The sharpening stone must have slipped,' he explained as Doyle worked. 'It shouldn't have. I was doing it right.'

Obviously, he hadn't been, but no one commented on the fact.

'That cut could do with a stitch or two, and you'll need a tetanus injection,' Doyle said.

Galadriel offered to drive Dai to the hospital, and when they had gone, Tamika and Doyle walked back to the scene of the accident to clear up the remains of the picnic.

Doyle picked up the big, heavy scythe. 'There's an art to sharpening these things' he said. 'Lucky not to lose his hand, never mind his thumb.'

Then, bending down and reaching into the long grass, he picked up the honing stone. 'I thought so,' he said. 'If you're canny, you soak these in water before you use them. They don't slip as easy that way, plus it makes them less likely to break if you drop them.'

'Is that something all policeman know, or just those from Ireland?' asked Tamika, smiling.

Doyle smiled back. 'I was brought up on a farm.'

'Well, anyway, thank you. God knows what would have happened if you hadn't been here.'

'I'm glad I was able to help.'

As they walked back to the house, Doyle said he needed to get on, so they agreed he would come again on Wednesday. By then he would have Sally's report and it wasn't as if anyone was leaving the country. So, taking Tamika's mobile number, he left, followed shortly by Tamika herself, who was anxious to resume her day off.

Galadriel took Dai to the casualty department and then home to his small terraced house in the town. She knew he lived alone: he'd told her so, often.

When she dropped him off, she said she would make sure his Land Rover was locked up and he could come collect it whenever he felt up to it.

Dai's thumb throbbed, but his brain throbbed even more now that he had time and solitude in which to think about the old well. Just how old was it? If it was anywhere near as old as it looked, he didn't need a dowsing rod to tell him there was money in it. How many tourists visited the Chalice Well every year? He bet it was at least half a million. And even if only half of them visited the new well and they only charged £1 admission . . . then there was the gift shop angle . . . he would talk to Maurice about it tomorrow. But right now, a stiff whisky.

~~~

Late afternoon sun bathed the grounds of Grey Havens as Granny Toogood made her way to her favourite flower bed. She was wearing her gardening clothes and blended into the shadows like a wraith. If anyone did happen to see her, they would just think she was doing a bit of weeding. In fact, she was tending the digitalis and aconite she had planted amongst a riot of other flowers in one of the untended beds. The latter was her favourite. Not so much for the lovely purple flowers as for its toxicity. Such a small amount of a carefully made tincture could kill. Even slight contact with the plant could cause the fingers of one's hand to become numb, which is why she wore gloves as she picked her lethal harvest and put it in a thick plastic bag. On her way back to the house she quietly sang the hymn 'We Plough the Fields and Scatter'.

Granny Toogood was not the only killer in the neighbourhood, however. As the sun set behind the looming mass of the Tor, other creatures hunted in the dark recesses of the ancient wood. Galadriel's cat, Bast, slaughtered everything that crossed his path, edible or not.

*Chapter 5*

Geoff Bendix hadn't just felt lucky on Saturday, he'd actually been lucky for a change. In fact, he'd made enough at Newmarket to pay not just his next instalment to Mr Smart, but also the back wages to one or two of his employees. Not all of them (he still had to fix the roof at Grey Havens for the new tenant), but there would be other races and he still felt lucky.

His father, Bert, was also feeling lucky, but for entirely different reasons. Tamika had driven over to Grey Havens and cajoled the old man out of his room.

'But it's not Sunday!' he had objected at first. 'And it's a bank holiday. The roads'll be clogged with tourists.'

'Never mind that. Daisy's in the car, it's her birthday, and for some reason she wants you to come to her party.'

'I hate birthday parties. Besides, it's too bloody hot out there. You can bring me a piece of cake tomorrow.'

'No show, no cake. Nor trifle, nor chocolate biscuits.'

'Oh, all right woman, stop yer moaning. Daisy's birthday, you say? How old is she?'

'Eight. Now do your trousers up.'

Bert got to his feet slowly, with all the 'oohs' and 'arrs' that are the refrain of advanced age and arthritis, then went to the large ornate dresser that took up almost one wall of the room.

With his back to Tamika he rummaged about in a drawer and put something in his pocket, then let her help him into his threadbare linen jacket.

The journey to Auntie Grace's small cottage in one of the back streets of Glastonbury didn't take long and he was soon sitting in an easy chair that had been brought out from the living room and placed under the shade of a garden umbrella. On a small table next to him was an ashtray and a cold beer. Auntie Grace, a large lady in a floral dress, came and sat down on a deckchair next to him. Bert was a white man from London's East End, and she was a black lady from Jamaica, but they got on well. They shared a common heritage of poverty. Both had suffered prejudices, albeit different kinds, that had scarred them in various ways. But neither of them had ever given up or given in. Cake was produced and 'Happy Birthday' was sung. Daisy brought Bert a large slice of cake and handed him a brightly coloured paper napkin adorned with the words 'Birthday Girl'. He put them on the table next to him and reached into his pocket.

'So, how old are you now?' He asked.

'I'm eight, said Daisy, as if eight was the best thing in the world to be.

'Can you count?'

'Of course, silly.'

'Count these, then' said Bert, and he gave her a handful of small, heavy gold coins.

She didn't know quite what to make of them. They didn't look like any other coins she had seen before, but they reminded her of those foil ones with chocolate inside, so she carefully bit one.

'Blimey!' said Bert, 'No need to test 'em, girl, they're real enough!'

Tamika and Auntie Grace looked at the treasure Daisy had been given. Eight gold sovereigns with the head of Queen Victoria on them.

'Bert, these are worth a lot of money,' said Auntie as the coins glittered in her hand. 'This is too much, surely.'

'Nah,' said Bert. 'Buy her something she needs, and with what's left buy something she likes. A bike perhaps. Every kid should have a bike, eh?'

Daisy sat on the grass at Bert's feet and ate her cake.

Presently she asked him, 'Are you a grandfather?'

She had heard about grandparents. They turned up in stories and on TV, and she knew some of her friends at school had them. She also knew she didn't.

Bert was sipping his beer when the question landed. Was he a grandfather? Not as far as he knew, anyway.

'No' he said, looking thoughtfully down at Daisy. 'No, I don't think I am.'

There was a silence and then Auntie Grace said, 'I bet if you ask nicely, Mr Bert will let you adopt him as a grandfather,' as if choosing aged relatives was part and parcel of growing up.

Daisy brushed crumbs from her face and climbed onto Bert's lap.

'I'll call you Grandad, then' she said. 'Did you get the gold from being a pirate?'

Auntie Grace laughed. 'Oh yes, he was a pirate, all right. And a highwayman, eh, Grandad?'

Bert thought about his own grandfather, a wicked old bugger if ever there was one, but the best kind a lad like him could have had. Grandpa Bob hadn't come back from the war, though, and all Bert had to remind him of the only member of his family who had ever showed any real interest in him was a faded photograph. His hand gently stroked Daisy's soft, dark hair. It was a hand scarred by time and countless fights; one that had not reached out with affection to any person, let alone a child, in many long, lonely years.

After a while, Tamika took Daisy to wash the rest of the cake off her face and make a fresh pot of tea.

'Go on and light up,' Auntie Grace told Bert, 'now the child is out of the way.'

He sat back, ferreted about for tobacco and papers, and produced a thin rollup. More a matchstick than a real cigarette.

Auntie Grace looked at it. 'Only seen a cigarette rolled that thin twice,' she said. 'Once just after the war, and once when my brother Winston got out of prison.'

Bert laughed, coughed a bit, then laughed again. 'Well, I have been a guest of her majesty's once or twice' he said. 'But nothing really serious. Just a bit of wealth redistribution, you might say.'

'Yeh, said auntie, ' just like my brother. He was a rogue, too.'

'Was?'

'Oh yes, gone now,' said Auntie, sad but resigned, 'like Tamika's mother. 'I'm the only one left of the ship generation.'

They talked of the past. Auntie Grace told Bert about her husband, a good man and fine cabinet maker who could only find work on the buses in Bristol.

'He was a bus cleaner, the lowest of the low, and stayed that way till he retired. I cleaned in the canteen until at last I got a job as a cook. We were never blessed with children of our own, but we had Tamika. And when we retired, we moved here and bought this place so he could finally have a proper workshop. He made all the furniture in the house. Three good years, we had.'

'And then?' asked Bert

'Cancer.'

The one word said it all. Illness and a long journey of pain for both of them.

Daisy came back outside then. She had put on a pair of bright yellow Wellington boots that were her current pride and joy. She asked Bert to tell her all about being a pirate and a highwayman.

'Did you take your horse on the ship when you went out pirating?'

Bert didn't know how to tell children's stories. He could tell wonderful tales to the police or the inland revenue, but small girls with big brown eyes, that was another thing entirely. So, Tamika wove the tales and Bert interrupted with details when he could think of any.

Finally, Daisy was put to bed and Tamika drove Bert back to Grey Havens. She helped him up the stairs (he refused to use the lift his son had provided) and waited while he got himself comfortable on his big sofa.

'Thank you,' he said. 'For making me go, I mean.'

Tamika patted his shoulder, then leaned over and gave him a brief kiss.

'Daisy loves you, Auntie likes you, and I can just about put up with you,' she said with a warm smile. 'I'll see you tomorrow. Sleep well.' 'Grandad'

~~~

Tuesday dawned as bright and sparkly as a film star's teeth. Tamika was pottering about the kitchen, Doris was hoovering aimlessly in the hall and still reluctant to go upstairs in case she met the ghost of Mrs Meldrum coming down. Galadriel was in her office. Formerly the library, this room had lots of rather nice mahogany bookcases that were currently filled with second-hand books that, along with Galadriel's cigarettes, gave the room a musty odour. It also had French windows that opened onto the rear garden. On the walls were celestial and occult charts, posters from past Glastonbury Festivals, and pictures of whales, porpoises, and restful scenes, each with a helpful message such as 'It's never as bad as you think' (under which someone, she was sure it was Bert Bendix, had scrawled in thick black marker, 'Yes it Fucking is'). Her large desk had a green leather top and lots of drawers, including a secret one, though she had forgotten where it was.

The only other furniture, apart from a cat basket, was Tamika's 'workstation'. Considering this was where the real work got done, there was a slight imbalance in facilities. Tamika's desk was an old kitchen table and chair. The desk held only a large mechanical calculator and box files, whereas Galadriel's was crowded with all manner of interesting rubbish, including a large ashtray now filled with the remains of the day. There was only one chair for visitors as the room was primarily for staff only. And Bast, of course.

Galadriel sat, cigarette in one hand, telephone in the other, desperately trying to speak with someone sensible at Glastonbury Police station. All she wanted to know was when she could have poor Mrs Meldrum's room back. She might just as well have asked for the meaning of life or the age of the universe down to the nearest week. She was getting the good old run around as uniform passed it to CID, and CID, who couldn't be arsed, transferred it to Traffic, who assumed she was enquiring about parking tickets. Frustration was no longer mounting; it was astride and galloping fast.

Things got worse. Outside one of the French windows, a spotty youth suddenly loomed into view and stood mouthing at her like a goldfish while brandishing a grubby business card on which was written 'Dennis Trimm, Reporter, South Somerset Recorder.' The *Recorder* was a local free rag whose readership was split between those seeking discreet intimate relationships and those looking for a good used fryer. It covered local events as well, mainly because of the need to fill space between the 'Friends Wanting Friends' pages and those advertising second-hand goods.

As Galadriel stared in fascinated horror at the spotty youth doing his goldfish imitation, there was a light knock on the door and, without waiting for a reply, Granny Toogood sidled in. She had been waiting impatiently for a chance to talk to Galadriel about moving into Mrs Meldrum's room. After all, that was the reason the old bat had taken her trip to eternity. She'd be alive now if she'd agreed to a room swap. Granny had tried talking sense into her, but she'd just got all uppity and spoke of celestial alignments and bloody 'feng shooey', whatever the hell that was. The fact of the matter was that Granny's own room was tiny and at the top of the house. It did have a small ceiling hatch that opened into the attic and this allowed her to store her 'equipment' by the huge water tanks, but this wasn't as secure as she would have liked. If she was out and some builder or plumber came up to attend to one of the catastrophes that seemed a regular part of life in this wreck of a house, then embarrassing questions might be asked. Meldrum's room was much bigger than Granny's, with more than enough room to hide her kit in, plus it was on the first floor, which would make it easier for her to slip in and out without being seen. Getting hold of Galadriel had not been as easy as she had thought it would be, however. The woman always seemed to be out.

Dennis Trimm, not having been shouted at to go away, began inching his way through the French windows. Immediately, it became a race between him and Granny as to who claimed the chair in front of Galadriel's desk. Granny won, and before her elderly arse even touched the seat she leaned forward, fixed her eyes on Galadriel's, and started talking. Dennis tried to turn defeat into victory by leaning on the desk and speaking louder than this feeble old woman.

In a matter of seconds, Galadriel had gone from one maddening conversation to three. Granny Toogood's eyes bored into hers while she rambled something about her room. The spotty youth leaned closer and closer, demanding answers to questions she couldn't understand. The voice in her ear told her to push various numbers for myriad incomprehensible options. Suddenly, she snapped. Smashing the phone down, she jumped up from the desk, screamed 'Fuck off!', and ran out of the room.

Her words were actually aimed at the reporter, but Granny took them to mean her as well. She reeled back as if she had been struck in the face. No one had spoken to her that way since she'd left prison. She was brought to her senses by Dennis.

He was young, desperate for a story, and quite unfazed by being told to fuck off. People told him to fuck off all the time.

Out came his notebook and pen. 'Someone fell down the stairs here last week and died; what can you tell me about it?'

Granny quickly recalibrated and looked up at him with all the pathos she could muster.

'Poor Mrs Meldrum. It was an accident. Haven't you anything better to do than bother us in our time of sorrow?'

Dennis was pleased because he now had a name to go with the headline he had already written in his notebook: 'Death on the Stairs, Police Baffled'. His normal investigative method was to keep on questioning someone until physically stopped, but something about this little old lady made him think better of it. Despite the woolly pink cardigan and the curly white hair, she somehow reminded him of Miss Roberts, his first primary school teacher. He went out the way he had come in.

Granny left the office and went up the stairs like a rat up a drainpipe. No respect! She was given no respect in this bloody place! If Galadriel only knew she had the privilege of housing one of the country's most successful mass murderers, she'd have a different look on her stupid face. Still cursing inwardly, she reached the top and cursed outwardly. At the best of times the landings were not well lit. Now the one dim bulb in the ceiling had gone out. That was always happening. The wiring in this place was a disgrace. As she stumbled to her room, her slippered foot came down on something squishy. Something squishy that nevertheless had a bit of crunch in it. Opening her door and turning on a light revealed this to be the remains of a rat that had been left outside her door. This frequently happened to other residents and she always rejoiced in their discomfort.

But now it had happened to HER. The culprit, of course was that fucking Bast (or, to those who had to share accommodation with him, 'Bast-ard'). When complained to, Galadriel always said they should regard it as a compliment as it was Bast's way of trying to provide for them. As if! Granny picked up the rat's mangled carcass with a piece of kitchen towel, walked across the landing, and threw it down the stairwell. That vile, malodorous, arrogant, fucking cat! She'd see to him.

She had just settled down with a nice cup of tea and some preliminary ideas for Bast's painful demise when the noise of pounding in the next room became unbearable. Gathering her knitting, she made her way down past workers carrying up roof tiles and timber. This meant Fatty Spratt's room was being made ready for a new tenant. The sooner she moved downstairs the better.

~~~

Galadriel had fled to her caravan. She would be safe from endless questions that had no answers here, she thought. She found the remains of a joint, lit up, and calmed down. After a while, she drifted into the garden to do a bit of harmonising with nature, then picked up her bike and cycled into town. She would have a coffee or perhaps a light lunch. Whatever. She was away from the house and that was the main thing. She was also nicely high, which was another.

Galadriel avoided the worst of the crowds by going down a narrow alley that led to a courtyard and The Happy Bean, a café run by a man known to all as 'Mung'. Because it was tucked out of the way and used mostly by locals, Galadriel knew she'd be able to find a place to sit. The acorn coffee and flapjacks satisfied her munchies, but when she went up to the counter to pay she realised that in her haste she'd forgotten to bring any money with her. The bill was only a few pounds and she was sure Mung would be fine with her popping in and paying it when she was next in town. The trouble was, Mung wasn't there and the woman behind the till was a stranger. As she feared, there was no expression of understanding on the woman's face as she tried to explain that she knew the owner, was a friend of his, in fact, and so on.

Things had reached an impasse when in strode Dai Griffiths. As soon as he understood the situation, he took his wallet out and thumped a twenty pound note down on the counter.

Then, taking Galadriel's arm, he said 'How about another coffee and a bun just to realign the old chakras?'

They sat down. 'That's very kind of you, Dai,' she said. 'I'm sure it would have worked out, but you know...'

'Don't be daft, girl. You'd have done the same for me. Blimey, we both go back a long way in this funny old town, eh?'

'How's your thumb?' asked Galadriel.

Dai held up his bandaged hand. 'Better, thanks. Thanks again for the ride to the hospital. Shame we never finished that picnic.'

Galadriel smiled and they chatted about mutual acquaintances: those who were interesting, those who were weird, and those who had moved on to become someone else. Dai purposefully did not bring up the subject of the room he wanted. Skirted around it as if it were a turd on the pavement, in fact, even when Galadriel said 'I tried all morning to get hold of the bloody police to find out when I can get poor Mrs Meldrum's room back.' Then she told him about the spotty youth who had crashed in.

'Oh, I know him' said Dai. 'A right little tit. I spend a lot of money advertising with that rag he works for, so I know the owner too. How about I have a quiet word and tell him that he'll get the full story when the police are through and not before?'

Galadriel was so relieved she reached across the table and put her hand on his, being careful of the big grubby bandage.

'That's really kind, Dai. I can't thank you enough. Look, there's still a lot to sort out. God only knows when the police will release the room and I have to get it cleared and find out where to send all the clothes and everything, but when I have, it's yours, okay?'

Dai didn't want to spoil the mood by asking how much and for how long, so he just smiled gratefully and put his hand over hers. He'd been sure she'd come around about the room in the end, but he was still pleased. Now he could concentrate on that mysterious well.

## Chapter 6

As a matter of fact, Mrs Meldrum's room was released the very next day. Doyle called Tamika to confirm she would still be available to answer his questions (a nice touch, she thought) and arrived mid-morning. Galadriel was happy for Tamika to deal with the police as she was already doing battle with Geoff and his builders.

Tamika and Doyle sat in the office this time. After the little incident with Dai and the scythe, Tamika felt more comfortable with him, but this was business. Doyle took out his notebook.

'I have the names of the people who were here when the deceased went down the stairs, but I need to know about the others who live here'.

Tamika noticed he said 'went' instead of 'fell', but let it pass. She had already prepared a list of the residents' names for him. She handed it over and he glanced through it.

'OK, this gives me their names, now give me their stories.'

'Well, starting on the first floor, there's Mr Bendix. He's the father of Geoff Bendix, who's a sort of partner in the business. His apartment is next to Mrs Meldrum's.'

'Yes, I remember him. He didn't have much to say besides "fuck off". So, he's Geoff Bendix's father. It's a small world, eh?' Doyle knew of Geoff Bendix in the way a good copper knows all the villains, major and minor, on his patch.

Tamika saw something in his expression that prompted her to say "He's an old man, in his eighties. A little gruff, sure, but very kind when you get to know him.'

Yes, thought Doyle, and the same was probably said about Attila the Hun.

'Mrs Spottiswood is in apartment 3,' Tamika went on. 'She's a widow in her late sixties, not much spare cash, apparently, so helps out where she can around the house. Big into the crystals and all that.'

'Has she been here long?'

'Since the beginning, really.'

'Right. Mr Tiptree, what about him?'

'NFG.'

'NFG?' asked Doyle. He'd not heard that one before.

'Normal for Glastonbury. A retired librarian. Had a long-time companion who passed away and now he spends a lot of time with his sister.'

'Where's that?'

'Wells. He's there more often than he is here. I think he doesn't get on with our cooking.'

Doyle made a note, then looked up to see Tamika smiling at him.

'I've never helped the police with their enquiries before,' she said. 'I was almost arrested once, though.'

He raised an eyebrow questioningly.

'Greenham Common. I was a student and went down with a group from university. Made a fuss but didn't actually achieve anything.'

'You can't know that for sure. And at least you tried to make a difference. That's what counts. What did you read at university?'

'Business Studies' said Tamika. 'Then parenthood happened.'

To prevent any further personal enquires, she said she would make them some coffee and left for the kitchen.

Shortly after Tamika returned, Granny Toogood left the summer house and approached Galadriel's office via the French windows. She wanted another crack at getting Mrs Meldrum's room and had even brought along some bed socks she'd just finished knitting as a gift. As she neared the office, she heard voices. Not Galadriel's, though. It was Tamika and someone else. Shit, it was that copper with the Irish accent. If she was any judge of coppers (and she was), that bastard was too clever by half. She took up a position where she could eavesdrop and still see if anyone was coming.

'On the second floor we've got Carmel Petalingo,' Tamika was saying. 'Now she's a bit weird even for Glastonbury. Tells everyone she's a direct descendant of the famous Gypsy fortune teller 'Romany Rose' but we once had a letter come addressed to a Miss Carmel Bludgeon. It had a Basingstoke postmark.'

'You don't miss much' said Doyle.

Tamika smiled and continued. 'Anyway, she's gone most of the summer, fortune telling on the pier in Blackpool.'

'I wonder if she could tell us how that old lady got down those stairs' he mused.

'Don't you think it was an accident, then?' asked Tamika, hoping it really was. Anything else was just too horrible to contemplate.

'Well, there's nothing to indicate it was anything other an accident, but you know how suspicious cops are.' Doyle grinned at her. 'Have there been any other deaths in the house?'

Outside, Granny stiffened and held her breath.

'Well, no, not actually in the house. Mrs Spratt, who lived on the top floor, died a few months ago, but it was while she was visiting her brother.'

'Do you know what happened?' he asked.

'She was asthmatic,' Tamika said. 'She had a really bad attack at her brother's and died. We were all very sorry. She was a lovely person, always singing, and really friendly to everyone.'

Doyle made a note to check up on this. It always paid to be thorough.

Tamika continued going through the list. 'Up on the second floor there's Mrs Prout-Smythe, a widow of private means. She's a Spiritualist and lives in India for months on end. Frankly, she can be a bit of a pain. In the room next to her is her sister, a Miss Langdolin. She's a couple of years younger, a retired teacher and keen birdwatcher. She's on a twitching holiday in Scandinavia right now. Much easier to get on with than her sister.'

The next on the list was Major Dennis Mottishaw.

'Yes, I remember him, too,' said Doyle. 'Nice old boy. A retired officer of the Green Jackets who served with the Ghurkhas. He told me all about his time in Nepal. How did he find this place?'

'His son saw an advert in one of the cafés in town. Major Dennis came back from Nepal when his wife died. He stayed with his son for a bit, but ultimately wanted his own place. It's his son who pays the rent here.'

'Must be doing well, then?' said Doyle.

'Yes, he's a music producer for the festival. Got pots

of money.'

'Right. Which just leaves Mrs Toogood. She knitted the whole time I took her statement and insisted on my calling her Granny.'

'Oh, yes, she's always called Granny and she's always knitting. In fact, that's pretty much all does; knitting and watching.'

'Watching?' asked Doyle

'Well, she has this favourite chair, you know, it's just an ordinary wing chair, and she moved it right into the corner of the room, next to the big bay window. It's opposite the door and she can see everything from it.'

'How do you know that?'

'I sat in it once when she was out. The light's good for reading there, so I suppose it's good for knitting, too. Anyway, she made quite a fuss when Mrs Meldrum tried to sit in it one morning.'

'So, they had a row?'

'No' said Tamika, 'nothing like that. Old people can get very possessive over little things. Like Mrs Spottiswood and her biscuits.'

'Does she go into Glastonbury at all? Does she have any friends or family there?'

'She goes into town sometimes. She doesn't have any family or friends that I know of.'

'Any letters come in for her?'

'None' said Tamika.

'I get the feeling there's something about her you're not comfortable with, though,' said Doyle. 'What is it?'

'Well, I don't really know how to explain it' said Tamika.

'She's too normal for Glastonbury. She doesn't drink, smoke, cast runes, or commune with the dead. Maybe that's why she watches us so much; we probably seem like very interesting people to her. To be honest, most of the time I think everyone just forgets she's there.'

Granny had heard enough. More than enough. How dare they! She, a successful serial killer, 'too normal' for Glastonbury? She, find all these self-important morons 'interesting?' She scuttled off, seething with indignation.

When Doyle left, Tamika found Galadriel and told her they could now access Mrs Meldrum's apartment. They agreed that packing her possessions was best done sooner rather than later. Tamika had called Mrs Meldrum's sister, who had said she would be putting everything in the hands of her solicitor. In the meantime, she requested her sister's belongings be boxed up and their safety ensured until they could be collected. That was about it. Short and not very sweet.

So, fortified with a few glasses of wine, Galadriel and Tamika spent a grim afternoon packing up the old lady's worldly possessions. Mrs Spottiswood tried to help but after umpteen stops to 'placate the spirits and harmonise the energies,' she was politely asked to take her crystals somewhere else. Doris said she'd like to help but had forgotten to bring her lucky rabbit's foot and without it the shade of the dead might follow her home. Major Dennis, however, was a star and made a detailed inventory of everything.

At last, only the furniture remained, and they covered that with dust sheets. It was a sad occasion; a whole life reduced to a few bundles that smelled faintly of lavender and strongly of moth balls. Galadriel was in tears as she locked the door.

'Is this what we all come to?' she sniffed.

'Only if we're lucky' said Major Dennis. He had seen many deaths, but very few easy ones.

Meanwhile, the building work progressed, but slowly. The timbers in the roof were rotten and the job was much bigger than had been anticipated. Piles of debris were accumulating outside the front door and Geoff, who didn't believe in paying to have things taken away, sent Desmond to find a suitable dumping ground in the garden.

Desmond was glad to be outside in the fresh air. Being a methodical young man by nature and at least partly an archaeologist by training, he quartered the grounds, making a small sketch map as he went. It took more time than he thought it would. He calculated there was something like three acres plus or minus huge hedges and a copse or two. This wasn't for Geoff's benefit; it was for his own enjoyment and to keep his hand in. After several hours, he was hot, tired, and almost lost. He had been stung by countless nettles and slashed by an enormous black cat. He wished he had a machete to deal with some of the undergrowth. Early in his explorations he had come across a pond that would have held a lot of rubble, but it was full of wildlife. A big toad had given him a knowing wink, so he'd decided to keep his trap shut about that option.

Eventually he came across the stone well Dai had spotted on Sunday. Desmond was enchanted. His instincts told him this was something special. He knew enough about medieval history to see that the stones nestling in their mossy bed were old. As old as the Abbey possibly, which was about three miles away on the other side of the Tor. On hands and knees, he examined the ground near the well and eventually found the remains of what could have been a building of some sort. Impossible to tell what sort without excavation and study, but Desmond still had friends at his University. He'd make some calls and find out what the records showed. As he made his way back to the house, he decided he would dump the rubble somewhere in Geoff's scrapyard. He'd never notice it amongst all the other rubbish.

~~~

On Thursday afternoon Dai had called unannounced and breezed into the kitchen through the back door. Tamika was preparing Bert's tea and regarded Dai's entry as an intrusion, but Galadriel's eyes lit up when she saw who it was. With a girlish giggle, she led him off to her office. Tamika rolled her eyes, thought 'Here we go again,' and took Bert's meal up to him.

In the office, Dai was all smiles and compliments.

'You look lovely, you should do your hair like that more often, what a nice office' and so on. Then the reason for the visit.

'Mabon's next month. Only twenty-two days away.'

Mabon is the holiday of the autumnal equinox, Harvest Home, and the Feast of the Ingathering. Like all pagan rituals marking the passing of the seasons, it is taken very seriously in Glastonbury, and the bounty of mother nature takes the form of mead, cider, wine, or beer. In fact, anything fermented that can be quaffed whist dancing around a fire to the beat of a bodhran.

'I don't think we'll do anything here' said Galadriel. 'Not so soon after Mrs Meldrum's passing.'

'Would you like me and the lads to do a quick astral realigning and cleansing ritual? Young brother Bladdwell has got hold of a fantastic ram's horn. Sounds bloody marvellous, it does.'

Galadriel declined the offer. She wasn't against Druidic rituals, but she'd hosted some in the past and they took a lot of cleaning up after. There were still stains on the hall carpet from the last one years ago.

Since his last visit to Grey Havens, Dai had been a busy man. He'd told his business associate, Maurice Grinder, about the old well, and Maurice, who was a retired schoolmaster with a BA Hons History, had been rather excited. Yes, it might be very old indeed. Right sort of place. The Chalice Well wasn't so very far away as the crow flies. That side of the Tor and all. But until the place could be checked out by a professional it was all just speculation.

So, Dai's current plan was to put someone into that spare room who could surreptitiously explore the site and tell if it were really real. Take photographs, nick a bit of stone, ferret about and find out. And of course without Galadriel knowing anything about it. If there was real money to be made out of the well, he wanted to be the one to make it.

Dai was a realist in Druid's robes, so you wouldn't have thought he'd be so surprised to learn that Galadriel was a pragmatist in her tie-dye and beads. The amount of rent she wanted was more than he'd anticipated.

'It's not me,' she said, 'Geoff sets the rates and he wants a hundred a week all in. He says it's cheaper than a boarding house.'

It was, thought Dai, but not by much.

'So, Geoff Bendix owns this place then?' he asked.

'Oh no,' said Galadriel, 'I own it, but I was in a bit of

trouble financially a while back and he put some money into the business so I could keep the house and not have to sell up.'

Dai was doing sums in his head. One hundred a bop for each room times fifty-two added up to fifty-odd grand a year gross. Not bad, but there must be a lot of expenses when you include wages and the like.

'All the rents are paid to him, then? Forgive me for being nosey, but well, you are a friend and I'd hate to see you getting turned over.'

'I'm not' 'said Galadriel, 'although there never seems as much money coming in as Tamika thinks there should be.'

'Your Tamika does the books, does she?'

'Just the household ones. Geoff has his own accountant. What with all his other business interests, you know. And, of course, he takes his loan repayments and . . . oh, what are those things called? No wait, I've got it, disbursements.'

I bet he bloody does, thought Dai.

'Well how about our little arrangement being in cash, paid directly to you?' he said. 'I mean, Geoff might get pissed off, but there's bugger all he can do about it, eh?'

'How much were you thinking of?' asked Galadriel doubtfully.

'Well, for a start you won't have to feed anybody. They'll come in, sleep, go out again, and they won't use the public rooms. Mabon is coming up, then Samhain of course, and Yule and so on, and in between times I have seekers signing up for the tours and many of them will be looking for somewhere to lay their weary heads after trudging the Ley lines and whatnot.'

'How much?'

'Let's have that calendar' he said, indicating the one hung

on the wall behind her.

She passed it to him.

'There are fifteen weeks, give or take, between now and Yule,' he said at last. 'How about I pay you eighty pounds a week, cash, up front, which would be, er . . . twelve hundred good old English pounds. How would that be?'

'No food, no frills, we just clean the rooms when they leave, and you guarantee any damage or loss?'

'Of course,' he said. 'And the fact is there'll be days when no one is staying in the room, but you'll still get paid. Paid in advance, like I said, cash in your pretty hand.'

Dai knew about the joy of cash in advance. It certainly beat promises from that crook Geoff Bendix. Their hands clasped; the deal was done.

Which was why, when Granny Toogood knocked on the office door and was at last able to ask Galadriel about Mrs Meldrum's room, she was told it had already been let.

Granny was furious. Her room, the one she had killed for, was now being let out to yet another fucking fruitcake! This was going to require her to teach someone a lesson. Suddenly she remembered Mrs Pettigrew and her precious Pekinese. The memory gave her some comfort. She had killed the dog, baked it in a pie, and fed it to the old cow. Then, knowing she had a dicky heart, told her about it just as she discovered her little darling's pink collar under the piecrust. Bang went her heart, and with no nitro-glycerine tablets to hand, either. Well, Galadriel might not have a dicky heart, but it would serve both her and that rat-killing bastard of a cat right if they got the same treatment.

Dai went straight to the bank and returned later with an

envelope stuffed with cash. Galadriel offered him a receipt.

'Were there bits of paper when the ancients built Stonehenge?' he asked airily.

'Bollocks' replied Galadriel. 'I don't want any misunderstandings about this arrangement.'

She called in Tamika, explained the deal, and asked her to write out a receipt for the cash. Tamika did so, without comment, but thought, 'There'll be trouble over this.'

*Chapter 7*

It was early September and a mist hung over the Tor, making it seem even more magical than usual. When Dai looked up at it from his bedroom window, however, all he saw was one bastard of a hill. And he was shagged out from walking up and down the fucker.

On the surface, he and his associates were fully paid up members of the New Age movement, but deep inside they were born again capitalists. Smells, bells, and mystic trances were one thing, but money in the bank was what mattered. They, like countless others before them, treated the whole spiritual herd as a source of income, like cattle or sheep. Milking would be gentle and regular, and fleecing would be discreet and leave no one feeling the cold. But it was big business and Glastonbury had been built on it. Ever since those cunning monks in the late twelfth century had 'found' the bones of King Arthur and Queen Guinevere, the place had been a gold mine for the Abbey; a money spinner that had only stopped when Henry VIII turned the place over. Pilgrims would come, spend what they could, and go away again happy in the knowledge that they were now a little bit closer to heaven. Dai and his fellow travellers were simply carrying on the ancient traditions.

Thankfully, there were no excursions that morning, so

Dai sat in his front room drinking real coffee (not the muck made with acorns he drank for public appearances) with Maurice and young Willow Walker (Charlie to his mum), making up 'seekers' purses'. Dai had invented these with an eye to his clients' fondness for spiritual talismans and tokens. They were small cloth bags purchased wholesale from a jewellers' suppliers (costing very little) that contained bits of ribbon to tie onto the Glastonbury Thorn as an offering to the old gods (costing almost nothing), mystic quartz pebbles collected by the bucketful from a beach in Wales (costing bugger all), and a small scroll of parchment-like paper with a few squiggles on it in the hand of Maurice Grinder. It was while this mundane assembly task was going on that Maurice told them he had done a bit of research on the well in Galadriel's grounds.

'Lots of references, nothing concrete' said Maurice, his delicate hands doing delicate things.

'So, it's not made of concrete, then' said Charlie.

'No, darling' replied Maurice, wondering how anybody as thick as Charlie could function, especially with all the weed he smoked. "It would appear that long ago there was at least one other well in that general vicinity believed to have had healing properties. Why or how it got lost or forgotten, one simply can't tell, but that's actually a good thing. If no one knows for sure, then no one can prove this well isn't that well. We just have to hope this one could be that well. Marketing will do the rest."

Dai then told them about the room at Grey Havens in which he could accommodate someone who knew their archaeology. Someone who would wander the grounds, quietly check it out, and report back.

When all the bags were made up, they went their various

ways. That afternoon Maurice was scheduled to act as tour guide for three elderly ladies from Milwaukee (one of whom was convinced she was a direct descendant of Guinevere), and Willow Walker was taking a party of young Australians around the Tor's mystic maze. Dai's job was to drive two retired couples from Cheltenham around the sacred sites, then back to their hotel for a good dose of his own special 'mystic healing'. At forty pounds a head, on top of the price of the tour. And, of course, everyone would get one of those rather special Seekers' Purses. Not a bad afternoon's business all round, and not a bleat out of the sheep as long as they were sheared discreetly.

~~~

Back at Grey Havens, Granny was seriously concerned the builders would discover the equipment and other kit she'd hidden near the big water tanks in the attic above her room. In addition to her distilling apparatus, she had accumulated a small cache of essentials she kept in a leather Gladstone bag. These included two books, one of which was *Mimms Formulary*. This tome described the uses of prescription drugs and, more importantly, their side effects. The other was much older and extremely rare. *Dame Nature's Tooth and Claw* was a small, leather-bound book with engravings that listed all the plants and fungi growing in the British countryside that could, in one way or another, kill. It had been published in 1887 by a Dr Erasmus Smollett whose research had led to the unfortunate deaths of his wife and four children, along with the cook and a housemaid. When their bodies were discovered, the book had been withdrawn from circulation and Dr Smollett lodged in a lunatic asylum, but the British Library had retained a copy.

Until Granny stole it, that is.

Also in the Gladstone were half a dozen pairs of 1950s vintage silk stockings (far superior to modern ones in making infusions), a brass knuckle duster, a small set of surgical instruments, three old-fashioned syringes and some extra needles, and a few bank books and passports. Last, but not least, there was an envelope full of faded newspaper clippings (most of them obituaries) she kept to cheer herself up when the pressure of having to hide inside some harmless little old lady got to be too much for her. Anything else she needed (large Kilner jars, coffee filters, and small glass bottles for the finished infusions) could be sourced locally. She moved the Gladstone bag to her wardrobe and locking it, hid the key.

If the builders were a bloody nuisance in one way, however, they provided an opportunity in another. Granny had been trying to work out a way to kill Bast without getting caught, having realized (once she'd calmed down) that baking him in a pie was probably not a safe option. Blaming his death on those oafs causing mayhem up on the roof, though, was too good a chance to miss. Her research had revealed that Doris fed the cat at roughly the same time every morning and Granny's window just happened to overlook the spot where she put the bowl. So, she stole a heavy lump hammer and awaited her chance.

It came the very next morning. From her perch high above, Granny heard the scrape of spoon on tin and Doris's calls of "here kitty, kitty" disturbing the peace. There was movement in the undergrowth, then Bast appeared on the lawn. He slunk towards Doris, who, knowing the spiteful beast of old, kept well out of the way of his lethal claws. When he began to eat the fishy sludge, she went back into the kitchen.

Granny leant out of her window, sighted, and let the hammer go. Silent death descended. It hit the ceramic food bowl, which exploded from the impact. Bast, startled and stung by bits of shrapnel, was otherwise uninjured and flew back to the bushes to take his chagrin out on the first living thing unlucky enough to cross his path.

Granny quietly closed her window and went inside to fume. 'Hell and damnation,' she thought as she took up her knitting, 'killing old ladies is a lot easier than killing that sodding cat.'

~~~

Desmond, to whom Geoff gave all the grot jobs, had unblocked the sink and was emptying the U-bend when Tamika offered him a cup of coffee. He gratefully accepted this and, while he was drinking it, asked her what she knew about the ruins in the grounds. Nothing, it seemed. It was a complete surprise. Naturally, she had explored the grounds with Daisy, looking for butterflies, bugs, and so on. But she had never noticed the well's ivy-covered stones. Galadriel came into the kitchen then and joined the discussion.

'I knew the well was there. I had it covered over years ago. It smelt really bad and I was worried Bast might fall in.'

'Well I think it's really old,' said Desmond, 'In fact, I suspect it's the same age as the Abbey. Do you mind if I do a little digging around it?'

'Don't make a mess, don't cost me any money, and keep Geoff out of it. Otherwise he'll have the stones for hardcore' said Galadriel as she walked away.

'Will it be all right if I bring a friend to have a look?' asked Desmond.

Galadriel just raised an arm in a sort of wave.

'I'd take that as a yes,' Tamika told him.

~~~

Later that week, Dai's Mystic Tours held its management meeting far from the madding crowd in a small pub deep in the Somerset Levels. On occasions such as this, Dai preferred to steer clear of the mystic fraternity in Glastonbury due to the fact that, in his experience, mystics were not very fraternal. They were always squabbling about which rituals were correct and whose staff of power was legitimate. Recently, a sage and a magus had come to blows over who had the right to a particular wand. It had really looked the business and was highly sought after until the eventual owner had paid to have the ancient Ogham script on it deciphered and learned it read 'Made in China'. Eventually he managed to sell it on to some newcomer to the craft for twice what he had paid for it. So much for spiritual solidarity. Dai occasionally tried to get a sort of trade association going in Glastonbury, one that would regulate what they all charged so there was no undercutting in the old shamanistic price lists. It never worked. There was always some bloody amateur who, once they had the wand and the crystals, would do the job for the price of a beer.

Consequently, he sought privacy and discretion when discussing business, and Mag's was a hostelry second to none for discretion. And cider. The latter aided in the former, actually, because visitors who partook of the ciders drawn from the cool, dark reaches of the back room rarely remembered their own names, never mind anyone else's.

Dai's business had enjoyed a profitable week, the weather

not having interfered with his schedule for once. It had been such a good week, in fact, that Dai brought the drinks without moaning. As they sat supping in a dark corner, Dai updated them on his Grey Havens scheme. He'd booked the room for four days starting on the 21st, which would give his spies a couple of days to look around after the Mabon celebrations.

'Who've you got, then?' asked Maurice.

'Sid and Megan Entwistle,' said Dai. 'Megan did an MA in Anglo Saxon plus all sorts of other useful stuff. Reads runes like you read the Racing Times.'

'Maybe, but Sid's a fucking weirdo' replied Maurice with some feeling. 'He's been banned from every coven and gathering from here to the Orkneys.'

'Why?' asked Charlie.

'Sid Entwistle, or "Cernnun" as he likes to be called, is a founding member of the order of Gnaddr', explained Maurice. 'Druidic serpent priests. He brought a couple of really huge boa constrictors to a Beltane festival near Milton Keynes a couple years ago. It attracted a lot of people and there he was, this tall, skinny bugger in robes with these snakes draped all over him. As he got nearer the sacred fire, though, the bloody snakes warmed up and got more active and the silly sod was so out of it he didn't even notice when one of them slithered off and wrapped itself around a small child. Parents went mental. Ambulance called, police everywhere, pandemonium all round. The locals blamed the ceremony for the heavy snow they had later in the year, and Sid and his snakes were banned.'

'He was known as Hissing Sid' after that,' said Dai. 'But he's calmed down a lot now. Hardly ever has visions, I'm told, and has given up the peyote almost entirely.'

'Well, you'd better hope Galadriel hasn't heard about him. She'll go mad if he brings his snakes.'

'Don't be daft' said Dai. 'They'll be Mr and Mrs Jones come to help with the Mabon celebrations, and I'm paying them so there'll be no reason for him to bring any fucking snakes.'

*Chapter 8*

It was a Monday. The Roman calendar indicated it was the ninth day of September in the year 1996. Mrs Spottiswood's calendar told her it was the month of the vine and today was dedicated to the Goddess Floramona, a minor Roman deity who brought luck to those wearing green. She put on a lime-coloured dress and decided to pop into town to try one of those lottery cards she had heard so much about.

For Tamika, it was just another Monday. There was the usual crop of bills and advertising rubbish, along with a postcard from Miss Langdolin. On the front was a picture of a small, grey bird looking pissed off. On the back was written 'Hope all is well, shall be returning 8th November.' Now that was kind, thought Tamika. Not at all like her sister, Mrs Prout-Smyth, who seemed to assume her intentions were somehow carried in the ether and was always irritated upon her return to find she had not been expected.

Miss Browne, the new tenant, was due to move in on Wednesday. She had been happy to keep Mrs Spratt's furniture, with the exception of the bed. Apparently, she had her own special orthopaedic divan and mattress, but apart from that she was just bringing her clothes, a lot of books, and of course her collection of houseplants. According to Mrs Spottiswood,

Miss Browne came from an academic background; her father had been Professor of Botany at University College London and as a child she had accompanied him on many of his plant-collecting expeditions.

'I first met her when she gave some lectures on medicinal plants to the Hampstead WI,' recalled Mrs Spottiswood, 'and then I found we belonged to the same church choir. After that she quite often joined my husband and me for a late supper after choir practice. I think she's just had enough of living in the big city and wants a bit of peace.'

Well, Tamika thought, let's hope we can provide that.

On Wednesday a small removal van turned up in the early afternoon. Miss Browne was in the passenger seat and the moment the vehicle came to a halt she leapt out and stood, hands on hips, looking around as if she were sizing up the situation. She had on an ancient anorak and a cloth hat of the sort worn by those who trudge the great outdoors, under which could be seen a shock of unruly steel-grey hair. A large nose drove a beaky wedge between two piercing eyes. These were violet rather than blue, and they shone with intelligence from amidst copious laugh lines.

Galadriel came out to welcome her.

'My friend Toby is helping me move,' Miss Browne told her, indicating the large, smiling Afro-Caribbean man sitting behind the steering wheel. 'And what a perfect day it is! I've been so looking forward to coming to Grey Havens.'

As she spoke, Mrs Spottiswood arrived on the scene.

'I've been looking out for you, Janet' she said. How was your journey?'

'It was fine, such lovely countryside!'

More pleasantries were exchanged and then the unloading began. The small divan was not a problem, the two small suitcases of clothes were easily handled, and the boxes of books required a little more effort, but the plant collection was something else altogether.

'Oh dear, I don't think I'll be able to fit them all in my room,' said Miss Browne. 'Will it be alright if I leave these on the landing for a bit while I sort everything out?'

When Granny Toogood returned from town and arrived on the top landing, she encountered a forest of vegetation, including some seriously large cacti. With difficulty she manoeuvred her way into her room to drop off her shopping and then went back down to see what she could find out about her new neighbour.

Over the course of the afternoon and evening, Miss Browne's plant collection overflowed into the kitchen, the dining room, and the common room.

'My plants need different conditions in which to thrive. Some like it sunny and some need a bit of shade,' she said. 'How fortunate that you have so many windowsills to accommodate them. I'm sure they're all going to be very content here.'

Granny, on the other hand, was far from content. Her chair had been moved away from the window to accommodate a monstrous spiky plant. Besides, there was something unsettling about the woman, though she had been perfectly charming when they were introduced.

'I'm so pleased to meet you! I hope I didn't cause you any problems when I was moving in. Tamika says you do a bit of gardening yourself. I do hope you will show me round tomorrow.'

Granny had done her best sweet little old lady act but was

already planning to have a sick headache next day.

~~~

Friday of that week happened to be the 13th of the month *and* there was a full moon, which caused both Mrs Spottiswood and Doris some consternation. Doris wore a sprig of willow and kept her lucky rabbit's foot in her pocket. Mrs Spottiswood lit a candle to St Ungulas, a crop of joss sticks to the Buddha, and a block of incense to the Lord of The Green as represented by one of Miss Brown's plants that had ended up in her room. The resultant smoke drove her out fairly quickly, but not before she had climbed on a chair and put a shower cap over the smoke alarm. She knew Tamika hated her to do this, but it was better than the bloody thing sounding off and Galadriel insisting everyone in the house go down to the front drive.

~~~

On Sunday morning, Desmond and his mate, Phil, came over to look at the well. Phil was a professional archaeologist who worked full-time for Taunton Museum and was bored out of his skull because he wasn't getting his hands dirty anymore. Tamika was in to collect Bert for lunch at Auntie's and noticed a strange van parked in the drive. Wondering who was there, she had a look round the back of the house and met Desmond and Phil on their way back from the well. They showed her some bits of pottery they had discovered. Phil thought the well probably had pre-Christian origins and, what was even more exciting, there looked like being a place of worship nearby. They wanted to wash some of their finds under the garden tap so went with Tamika to the summer house where Bert was waiting for her, having a smoke, and reading a magazine left behind by Mrs Spottiswood.

'Would you fucking credit this!' he barked when the trio entered. 'For a few quid Mystic Maureen will read your future from your handwriting, and for a few quid more will advise you on your prospects in love, marriage, and personal development along the astral plane. What a load of bollocks!'

If he was unimpressed with the services Mystic Maureen offered, he was agog with indifference when it came to small, dirt-encrusted pieces of pottery.

Phil smiled and held one out to him. 'Go on,' he said, 'hold it. Don't be afraid of the dirt.'

'Afraid of the fucking dirt! Lad, I've had more dirt under me fucking fingernails than you've ever shovelled in yer life, yer cheeky sod.'

But he did hold the small, squarish object and looked closely at it as Phil told him that, in all probability, this was a fragment of an encaustic floor tile, probably fourteenth century, and possibly made in Wells, where a medieval pottery had been excavated.

'It's not top quality,' he said, 'but it's undoubtedly ecclesiastical. In other words, that well site is of historical interest.'

Bert held another even smaller piece of greyish ceramic. This, he was told, was possibly a fragment of medieval pottery, same sort of date. Surprisingly, it all seemed to fascinate the old man and they were in danger of being late for Sunday lunch. Tamika reminded him of this and was helping him get up when she mentioned to Desmond how difficult it was for Bert to negotiate the stairs.

'He still refuses to use that stairlift. You might as well take it away when you get a chance. Nobody else uses it, either.'

Desmond asked if another handrail attached to the wall would help. Phil said that's what his grandmother had, and it worked for her.

'Sounds like it would be worth a try,' said Tamika. 'I'll ask Geoff about it one day if I can catch him in the right mood.'

As he painfully folded himself into the front seat of Tamika's car, Bert turned to Desmond and Phil and said 'You keep in touch. I'm not as old as what you're digging up, but that don't mean I'm not interested. All right, lads, now fuck off back to yer hole and see what else you can find. Maybe some gold, eh?'

And, still laughing, he was driven away to Sunday lunch with his newfound granddaughter who, he was sure, would have her own ideas about buried treasure. He looked forward to discussing them with her.

When Tamika brought Bert back to Grey Havens at six that evening, they found the stairlift gone and a very serviceable handrail fixed to the wall on the flight of stairs that led up to Bert's landing. It made a big difference and they were both grateful.

~~~

On Monday, Doyle called by. He and Tamika sat in the kitchen, having a brew up. Lowering his voice to ensure he wouldn't be overheard, Doyle asked 'Was anyone here close to Mrs Spratt? Anyone she always chose to sit next to or accompanied on shopping trips?'

That took Tamika by surprise. She thought he was here to discuss Mrs Meldrum, not someone who had died months earlier.

'Well, she was generally popular. Used to be a singer of some kind. Professional, you know, sang in operas, things like that. She still sang a lot. In the bath, in the garden, and I think in a choir in town. I don't know that she had any particular friend here, though, not really. She got on with everybody.'

'There was no one she argued with? Someone who didn't like her singing in the bath? You told me that in places like this you're bound to get tensions. Tiffs, you know, getting on each other's nerves.'

Tamika laughed. 'They're old hippies,' she said. 'Old age doesn't mean you can't be New Age. Oh, they don't all wear beads and burn incense but they're a pretty laid-back bunch. The only "normal" or "typical" old people living here are Bert Bendix and Granny Toogood. What about poor Mrs Meldrum, though? I thought that was why you were here.'

Doyle paused then said, 'I went to see Mrs Spratt's brother. Nothing official, but just because I was curious. He's a nice guy and devastated about his sister. She had visited lots of times before and yes, she was asthmatic and had to be careful, but she always had her kit with her. He was in his shop, maybe half an hour, no more, and came back into the house to find her literally breathing her last. He really beats himself up over it.'

'Poor man' said Tamika. 'That's terrible. Didn't she have her inhaler with her?'

'That's just it' said Doyle. 'Her brother said that while she could be a bit dotty at times, forgetful over names and the like, she always had her inhaler with her. And she had actually had two of them with her this time, but they were both empty. Or if not actually empty, there wasn't enough medicine in them to do her any good.'

'Were you able to see them?'

'Gone. Taken with her in the ambulance.'

'And the police? Were they called?

'No. Officially she died in the ambulance of a known cause, so there wasn't even an autopsy.'

Tamika looked so alarmed and unhappy that Doyle added 'There's no evidence of foul play. And there's no known motive. That's why I asked if she'd rowed with any of the other residents. Something is not quite right,' he added with a wry smile, 'but it may just be me. Probably been in the job too long.'

'Well, now that you mention it,' said Tamika slowly, 'I seem to remember Granny did once make a bit of a fuss because Mrs Meldrum's singing was disturbing her.'

Doyle's eyebrows raised at that.

'But it didn't amount to anything,' she continued. 'Major Dennis calmed them down and that was the end of it.'

'Probably. But Mrs Toogood was also at home the day Mrs Meldrum died. I'd like to have a chat with Major Dennis.'

'Of course,' said Tamika. 'I'll go see if he's available.' She returned shortly and led the way to the Major's room.

Doyle and the Major had much in common. Both men had seen action against implacable enemies and still bore the scars. No one but a fool displays their scars, physical or mental, but those who bear them can see them in others. Despite this, however, Major Dennis could add nothing to Doyle's investigation. He admitted he'd been asleep, deeply so for some reason, on the morning of Mrs Meldrum's demise. As for Mrs Spratt, she had been very asthmatic. Always had her kit with her. Why it had been empty at her brother's, it was impossible to know. Yes, there had been a small skirmish between her and Granny Toogood about noise (not everyone was a fan of opera), but it had been nothing serious and was never, to his knowledge, repeated.

Doyle was mildly disappointed but not surprised. Tamika offered to make him some lunch, so they returned to the kitchen, where she was relieved to find he could converse about something besides suspicious deaths. She found herself chatting happily about how she'd come to work at Grey Havens and the unexpected friendship with Bert.

'Do you have much to do with his son, Geoff?' asked Doyle.

'Not if I can help it. His father doesn't have much time for him, either. I think Geoff pulled a fast one moving him in here. Bert had a house in London and Geoff's renting it out or trying to sell it or something. He certainly always seems to be short of cash when it comes to paying bills and making repairs.'

'I think you're wise to be wary of Geoff' said Doyle. 'He's got a bit of form. Nothing serious, but let me know if he causes you any problems.'

~~~

On Tuesday morning it was pouring with rain. Doris had just cleaned the hall when the front door burst open and the robust figure of Carmel Petalingo appeared, lugging in two huge suitcases and a great quantity of dirt from the drive. Her ample form was draped with an old army poncho, making her look like a mobile yurt. Leaving muddy footprints and her dripping cases behind her, she went to the kitchen for a much-needed coffee. Tamika was clearing up the breakfast things but put on a fresh brew and listened as Carmel recounted her sad tale. Blackpool had been slow, not many punters, and the weather hadn't helped. Her usual digs had been taken over, so she had had to find somewhere else to stay. It had taken her ages. Then she had trouble with the car. Then she had lost her address book, which meant she couldn't contact her regulars and had to rely on passing trade. And so on.

As she unloaded her woes, Tamika thought 'This lady is a professional fortune teller. One who read the stars, the cards, and possibly even the entrails of chickens. She has earned her living for God knows how long predicting the futures of others, yet here she is, soaking wet, probably broke, having experienced myriad troubles she apparently could not foresee.'

Tamika told her about Mrs Meldrum and Carmel replied sagely that she'd had a message from across the void, so was not entirely surprised.

'And we have a new resident on the top floor. Her name is Janet Browne and she's responsible for all the lovely pot plants everywhere. We didn't put any in your room as you were away, but I'm sure she could spare one or two if you'd like them.'

The following morning Carmel had recovered her natural good humour. She was pleased to be home and immersing herself in the multicultural pond that was Glastonbury. Besides, Mabon was just a few days away and she was looking forward to a good bash.

So was Mrs Spottiswood. Margery Glossop, her friend and fellow member of the Sacred Sisterhood of Matronae, was coming to stay with her. Mrs Glossop was actually a high priestess of the order, so it was quite an honour to host her for Mabon. Unfortunately, that lady never left home without her aged miniature poodle, Mani. Mani was named for the Norse god of the moon, but of course everyone just thought his name was 'Manny.' Any charm Mani may have had as a puppy was now long gone. Years of overindulgence had turned him into an obese, snappy, yappy nuisance whose breath would stun an ox. But as all dogs gave Mrs Spottiswood runny eyes and the sneezes, arrangements had been made for him to stay in the ashram, so that was all right. Nominally of the masculine gender, Mani would not in any case have been permitted to accompany his mistress during her worship because the Sacred Sisterhood was a strictly female society. Its adherents were ladies whose days of dancing around 'sky clad' were well and truly over, but who still liked to dress up for a bit of gentle cavorting, with a nice piece of cake and a sherry or two afterwards. Galadriel was also a member, but not as dedicated as Mrs Spottiswood and her friend Margery, who knew all the words to the chants.

As it turned out, lodging Mani in the ashram was all right for everyone except Mani and Major Dennis. Mani was not used to being excluded from Margery's society, and continuously barked his displeasure at this arrangement. As he had an extremely shrill bark, fifteen minutes in Mani's society was enough to convince Major Dennis a strategic retreat was in order. He couldn't abide little dogs. Never saw the point of the things, so he went to stay with his son for a few days, hoping that by the time he returned the nasty creature would have left Grey Havens.

Miss Browne was settling into both Grey Havens and Glastonbury very well. Within a week she had joined the local garden society, a choir, and a book group. She also spent time exploring the grounds, saddened by the neglect but delighted to discover some very old apple trees as well a few interesting shrubs. Galadriel was only too pleased to hand over the garden maintenance to her with the reservation that there wasn't any money for plants.

'That won't be a problem, my dear, there's more than enough to be getting on with. I missed having a garden in London so it's a joy to get my fingers in the earth again, and I expect some of the other residents would like to have a go. We could even grow some veg; it's a bit late in the year now to plant much but we can cultivate an area to have ready for the spring. For now, I'll just determine what's worth keeping and do a plan for you to look at. I know you'll be busy for the next few days with the Autumn festival, so I'll keep out of your way until the dust has settled.'

On Friday, Dai dropped by to tell Galadriel who would be staying in 'his' room and that they wouldn't need feeding or cause any bother.

'You won't know they're there, you won't' he said to her. 'Lovely couple. Retired teachers. Nice and quiet, just here for the ceremony plus a couple of days to see the sights and all that.'

The 'lovely couple' creaked up the lane the following day in a tatty camper van. They were greeted by Galadriel, who thought they had quite a lot of luggage for such a short stay: a picnic basket, a backpack covered in festival stickers, and three cases, one very large. The man struggled up the stairs with the large one, which was a huge, soft-sided affair.

'It's all our robes for the ceremonies,' he explained. 'We're really looking forward to it.'

Once they were in the room, Galadriel examined her guests. The woman was a homely and comfortable looking soul, dressed in a tie-dyed garment with obligatory beads and amulets, her grey hair gathered in beribboned dreadlocks. She would fit in

Glastonbury without murmur or mantra. The man was tall, very thin, heavily bearded, and wore a black, long-sleeved shirt and ragged jeans with patches. They seemed friendly enough and introduced themselves as Megan and Sid Jones. Galadriel pointed out the tea making facilities, said she had left a bottle of fresh milk in the fridge, and left them to it. She thought they seemed like a nice enough couple.

As soon as Galadriel left, they sprang into action. Sid put the huge case on the bed while Megan prepared the bathroom. The side of the case began to move, as if something inside were undulating. Sid went to the picnic basket, carefully opened the lid, and took out a wriggling white mouse. Holding it by the tail, he cautiously unzipped a corner of the case. A long, triangular reptilian head poked out and seem to smile, holding the mouse by the tail, he dropped it in the open maw.

The case contained Mabel, the other woman in Sid's life. She was a huge boa constrictor. Sid knew that if Dai found out he'd be furious and refuse to pay the £200 for the job, but she'd been brought along because they'd taken a booking for an exhibition ceremony to be performed for the Pilton WI on the day after Mabon. These WI gigs could be worth a few quid provided travel expenses were kept down. So, he and Megan were looking forward to a paid holiday in the West Country, courtesy of Dai's Mystic Tours, and then earning a bit extra on the way home. Mabel was transported in a vivarium Sid had installed in the camper van. It even had battery-powered heating pads that sometimes worked and sometimes didn't. Right now, they didn't and, not wanting to leave her in the van overnight without them, Sid had used the enormous case to get her up to their room. Later that evening Dai collected Sid and

Megan and took them out for dinner. Mabel lay in the bath, slowly digesting the mouse and dreaming of jungles.

~~~

Up in her room, Granny had been busy. With due care and at great personal risk she had infused her aconite in proof spirit. It was lucky for her the builders had not spent long in the attic and never needed to access the area in which she had hidden her equipment. It was not so lucky for the bats who slept above this apparatus and lacked the WWII gas masks and long rubber gloves, which was what she used for her own protection.

Observation and patience are everything in a hunter, and Granny had them both. After the fiasco of the falling hammer she had followed the cat's movements with the same attention to detail as a famous television naturalist, but without the mellifluous tones. The animal was fed twice a day and, in the summer, always outdoors. His bowls had been relocated to a sheltered spot under the eaves of the Summer House near the orchard. The foul beast sometimes took the sun in the middle of a flower bed nearby, and when it rained, he retired to Galadriel's caravan, which had a cat flap. Otherwise, he patrolled everywhere at will, including within the house, but at no particular time, so there was no point lying in wait somewhere with an edged weapon or a blunt instrument. Poison, then, was the answer. It was silent, left no obvious mark, and, in this particular case, there was no danger of a post-mortem. Thus, Granny's personal celebration of Mabon had involved the purchase of a very expensive tin of cat food. Her lethal tincture was then added to the succulent meat lumps. 'From the gravy to the grave,' she chuckled, as she doctored the pungent mass.

~~~

Sid and Megan were the first up on Sunday morning. Sid was a bit hung over from their evening out with Dai, but Megan helped him wrap Mabel in a duvet cover and he crept downstairs and out to the camper van, which was parked in a perfect spot in the orchard, in the shade and out of sight.

Margery Glossop came down a little later and went to the ashram to see if her 'precious lovely boy' had had a good night's sleep. Mani was given a quick trip around the garden to 'do his business', a fresh bowl of water, and a packet of dried treats. Then, with a cushion to nap on and his lead tied to a chair leg, he was left.

As the morning progressed, preparations for the autumnal equinox celebrations began in earnest. Being a real pagan takes effort. You don't just wander into a church, sit down, and wait for it all to happen. You have to work for it. Woading up takes time and making headdresses of leaves and branches requires skill and a lot of hair pins. Robes have to be ironed and donned, badges of office and suitable talismans applied, and of course a wand is essential.

When all the worshippers had set off to their various festival celebrations, Granny got out her specially prepared bowl of cat food and, carrying it in a plastic bag, went down the stairs and out into the garden. She walked quickly across the lawn to where Bast's dishes sat in their halo of flies and carefully placed her bowl of tasty morsels in prime position. Then she went to the kitchen, made herself a cup of tea, stole two of Mrs Spottiswood's special biscuits, and humming a merry tune, retired to her room.

All was well in the lush, green garden that September day. Bees buzzed about their business, birds twittered and sang, and all nature seemed content. All except Mabel, that is. The travelling vivarium was nothing like as roomy as the one she had at home. It also had a loose clasp on the lid. Mabel made a slow, graceful exit from the plexiglass box and lay tasting the air with her tongue. It was coming from the camper door which Sid in his crapulence had neglected to close properly. She slid through it and down into the luxurious grass. A gnarled old pear tree nearby offered some sturdy, low branches to climb. She slithered up, draped herself comfortably, and became invisible.

~~~

Everybody thought the Mabon celebrations went as well as could be expected. The weather was fine, and the various groups, covens, and pagan fraternities put on a good show. There were no major incidents, though the collision of the Druidic Order of the Sacred Path with The Earth Mothers Convocation halfway up the Tor caused a bit of ill feeling and some minor damage when the cymbals of one collided with the symbols of the other. The marshals who choreographed the procession blamed the Earth Mothers for being late, and the Earth Mothers blamed the musicians for upsetting the energies. The sun set and the festivities continued in the pubs and around the bonfires. Dai's Mystic Tours had done exceptionally well. Dai had a full complement of seekers and they certainly found things, whether they had sought them or not, and at a cost that was not unreasonable, all things considered.

~~~

Meanwhile, back at Grey Havens, Mani sat discontentedly on a damp cushion that smelled of cat. He'd eaten all his treats hours ago and he was hungry. He could smell a proper meaty snack not too far away and, growling with frustration, worried the lead with his small, sharp teeth until it finally gave way. He pushed at the ashram door with his head and was pleased to find it opened out. Freedom and food were at hand! Following his nose, he soon came upon the bowl of pungent meat in its slimy gravy and scoffed the lot. Fairly soon he didn't feel at all well. He managed to stagger along the flower bed for a yard or two before collapsing under a pear tree. Mabel looked down upon his convulsions with interest. Her mouse had been some time ago and she was peckish. She looped down and wrapped him in her deadly embrace. His twitching stopped.

Granny had spent most of the day peering from her window down into the garden but had seen no movement nor heard any howls of distress. At dusk she could stand it no longer and crept through the empty house and out into the garden. She went towards the ashram and, yes, there was the bowl, on its side, empty! She grinned and looked around for Bast. She didn't find him in the garden, so she checked inside the ashram. There was no sign of him. Finally, peering through the grot-encrusted windows of Galadriel's mobile home, she saw him curled up motionless on the bed. Oh hurrah, she thought, dead on her bed, what a result! She danced a silent jig and Bast, sensing the movement, opened one disdainful eye and yawned hugely, displaying a mouthful of large, sharp teeth.

Granny was rigid with shock for a few seconds, then automatically looked around for a weapon. She could find nothing to hand, and anyway the caravan door was locked.

'I'll get you yet, you, bastard cat,' she snarled. 'See if I don't!'

Then the sound of a car approaching the house made her scurry indoors and up the stairs to her room.

Mabel, back in her pear tree, was slowly digesting her meal. As night came on the temperature dropped and she decided it was time to seek a warmer spot. She slithered down the tree, through the long grass, and towards the building. The door to the basement was ajar, and so she went down some stone steps and into the laundry room. Mrs Spottiswood had wandered off halfway through folding her clothes and left the dryer door open. The light inside reminded Mabel of her vivarium so she climbed in and made herself comfortable amidst that lady's woollen vests and formidable bras.

An hour or so later Sid returned. He had had a long day and a tiring one. Much dancing, gesticulating, and chanting had fair worn him out. He was not as young as he had been, and the old druid robes and headdress didn't get any lighter. He got a second wind, though, courtesy of adrenaline when he found the door of the camper van open, the vivarium top ajar, and Mabel missing. It wasn't as if he could ask the other residents to help look for her, either. She was his guilty secret.

The search for Mani had begun some time earlier. When Margery got back to Grey Havens, she had gone straight to the ashram to be reunited with her 'four-legged little man' but had found only the remains of his lead. She was already hysterical when she joined the others in the kitchen. Mani was not one to roam, she wailed. He hardly ever went out into the big wide world, and when he did it was with her and on a lead.

They all tried to calm her down and promised to help look for him. Galadriel got her some tea and Mrs Spottiswood did a very detailed search using the pendulum and an ancient ordnance survey map, which indicated Mani was in Salisbury, or possibly Shepton Mallet.

While everyone else wandered aimlessly about the grounds shouting the dog's name, Margery borrowed a torch from Tamika and walked along the lane, carefully checking the verges and peering into the hedges, until she came to the main road. The traffic was light but very fast, the headlights almost blinding her as the cars sped by. She knew Mani had never walked this far in his life, but still she made herself go up and down both sides of the road looking for but dreading the sight of a small white splatter of canine roadkill.

Finding none, she was making one last search around the back of the house before giving up for the night when she ran into Sid. His hunt was taking him both along and up. He knew the along probably wouldn't be very far, but the up was a right bastard. As she watched him shine his torch into the foliage of each tree, Margery thought he was very kind to help so enthusiastically, but for the life of her couldn't understand why he was wasting time this way. Mani couldn't climb trees.

Sid had learned of Mani's disappearance from the other searchers, so he knew Margery had been souring the countryside. Desperation made him ask her if, during her searches, she had perhaps noticed a snake anywhere about.

'A snake!' she gasped. 'How big a snake?'

Sid held his arms out to indicate 'quite big.'

'Big enough to swallow a dog?' she managed.

Sid gave a sort of shrug and mumbled through his vast beard, 'Boa constrictor.' He added quickly, 'Very friendly! House trained! Safe with kids and pets, honest!'

Hell hath no fury like a woman who has lost her dear little doggie and finds he's been gobbled up by a fucking great boa constrictor. Grabbing Sid by the beard, she rained blow after blow on his head with her torch. The screams brought the others quickly onto the scene, where they found Sid in a heap on the ground. Eventually they managed to pry Margery off him, and Galadriel took her, sobbing, to the kitchen.

Tamika helped Sid to his feet and led him indoors, where Galadriel was doing her best to comfort a still weeping Margery. Placing Sid as far away from them as possible, she attempted to find out what the hell was going on. It took half a roll of kitchen towel, several shots of brandy, and some of Mrs Spottiswood's biscuits before the facts could be dragged out of the combatants.

Sid assured everyone that Mabel had been fed only yesterday. 'Boa constrictors only eat every couple of days,' he said, 'and only mice at that.'

Tamika thought it highly likely the bloody snake had eaten the sodding dog but didn't like to say so. 'I suggest we wait until daylight to continue the search,' she said. 'Major Dennis will be back by then and he was a trained hunter. He lived in jungles and probably knows all about snakes.'

Sid protested loudly. 'My Mabel is a protected species! There's no way I'm going to let anyone hunt her down! She's innocent, I tell you!'

Tamika sent him upstairs to his wife, who had been oblivious to all the goings on thanks to a bag of skunk Charlie Willow Walker had sold her that afternoon.

Between them, Galadriel and Tamika got everyone bedded down eventually. Tamika went home exhausted and Galadriel went to her bower, where she lay and stared at the fairy light constellations above her bed and wondered what the hell she had done in a previous life to deserve all this.

At last, only one window in the house showed a light. Granny sat on the bed and chewed her fingers. Wearing a fluffy pink bed jacket over a demure Winceyette nighty with a ribbon hem, she looked every inch the stereotypical sweet little old lady, but inside she was the human equivalent of molten lava. Seeing Bast alive and well on Galadriel's bed had been bad enough but coming back to her room and finding that the vile, evil, nine-lived monster had crapped on the carpet outside her door really was the last straw.

~~~

Margery was up with the dawn next day and walked as far as Geoff Bendix's scrapyard looking for some trace of Mani. She found none, however, and returned to Grey Havens, anxious and sad, to see if there had been any sighting of him at the house. It was the not knowing that was so hard to bear.

Sid was also out searching, but with just as little success. Neither he nor Margery spoke when their paths crossed, and he kept well out of striking distance in case she started on him again.

Mrs Spottiswood came down for breakfast rattling on about what the crystal pendulum had shown and how it was never wrong. Even Granny Toogood was red-eyed and tired over her breakfast. Tamika put that down to the loss of Mani. Perhaps she was the sort of old lady who liked spoiled little doggies.

Major Dennis arrived just after 9:00 and Tamika told him the whole sorry tale over breakfast. He sat munching his toast, eyes bright, moustache bushy with excitement.

'The snake has undoubtedly eaten that dog. I saw it often in Burma. Damned constrictors took small animals, even children if they could get them. Wily beasts. Where have you looked?'

'All over the grounds, and Mrs Glossop even went up to the main road last night, but there's been no sign of either animal.'

Wiping the crumbs from his lips, Major Dennis stood up and said, 'I'll go to my room and change. Meet me in the hall in ten minutes.'

From the garden came the lonely cry of 'Mani! Mani!' as poor Margery searched amongst the foliage once more. Up and down the stairs and in and out of his camper Sid wandered in search of his Mabel. Granny murmured something about laundry and headed for the utility room with a bag of clothes.

Major Dennis arrived wearing an old bush jacket and carrying a cricket bat. He raised this in a quick salute and, before Tamika could think of anything to say, darted off into the grounds.

In the gloomy and now slightly steamy utility room, a washing machine rumbled, hissed, and churned. The air condensed on the tiles and the vibrations increased as the ancient appliance staggered through its cycle. Granny went to clear the dryer. That damned Spottiswood woman has taken off in the middle of doing her laundry again, she thought as she reached in, gathered up the clothes, and dumped them on top of some folded ones in a basket.

Suddenly, Mabel was exposed and vulnerable. She was also having real trouble digesting Mani. Instinct took over. When a boa constrictor's stomach is full and danger threatens, the established protocol is a good projectile vomit. Granny, checking to see she'd got everything out of the dryer, got the slimy, stinking remains of the little dog full in the face. She screamed as she had never screamed before while Mabel exited the dryer and slithered into the darkest spot she could find, which was a wall behind a massive mangle.

The first on the scene was Tamika, who froze at the sight of Granny Toogood trying to wipe something wet, furry, and nasty off her face with a pair of bloomers. Next came Sid, rapidly followed by the Major who, seeing Granny dripping with the remains of some half-digested animal, raised his bat and slowly advanced into the room. Sid scurried around, frantically looking in all the places a frightened snake might hide. There weren't that many, and he soon found Mabel. She was alive, thank all the gods, she was alive! He turned to find something to wrap her in and was confronted by the Major.

'Move out of the way, man, those things are dangerous!' he shouted, flourishing his cricket bat. 'Leave it to me, I'll bag the blighter!'

'Noooo!' wailed Sid, his long, skinny arms stretched out to shield Mabel. 'She's tame! She's mine!'

Tamika attempted to take control of the situation. She told Major Dennis to put the bloody bat away and go find Galadriel. Just then, Margery, drawn by the sound of excited voices, ran into the room. The scene that met her eyes would haunt her for the rest of her life. A small, elderly lady whose face appeared to be covered in snot and pea soup was retching and clinging to a wildly vibrating washing machine. At her feet was a small bundle of skin and bone with a few moist strands of white fur curled around it. Despite its awful state, she recognized this immediately as the remains of her dear, sweet Mani. She rushed over, grasped the putrid object, then fled the scene shrieking and clutching it to her bosom.

Tamika attempted to help Granny Toogood remove her noisome cardigan, murmuring words of comfort such as 'bath' and 'back to bed'. Suddenly the china blue eyes that had seemed so far away hardened into sapphire. Granny straightened up and, without a word, walked out of the laundry room.

Sid gently coaxed Mabel into an old sheet he'd found. She seemed glad to be there and didn't move while he carried her out to the van. He and Megan would be leaving just as soon as they could pack up. Sod Dai and his stupid ancient well. They'd lose the £200, but Mabel had been through enough.

The remains of Mani were washed under the tap in the garden and swathed in a large silk shawl donated by Galadriel. This did nothing to placate Margery, who bawled that as soon as she got home, she would be contacting the constabulary, the RSPCA, the environmental agency, and her solicitor. Nothing anyone could say made any difference; the woman was bent on revenge.

Galadriel had had enough. She telephoned Dai Griffiths.

'Peace, harmony, and light' he answered in silky tones. 'Dai's Mystic Tours, how can I help you?'

'I'll tell you how you can help me, you, Welsh git,' shouted Galadriel. 'Don't send any more lunatics with huge fucking snakes to my house!'

At the word 'snakes', Dai's blood had gone cold. 'What's happened?' he asked, holding the phone an inch or two from his ear.

'Your guests brought their pet snake with them! A bloody great boa constrictor that got loose and ate a visitor's dog!'

'Oh, my dear, poor you' he said, his lilting Welsh accent

dripping with sympathy. 'You've had a horrible time. I'll come right over, and you can tell me all about it.'

He had to listen to her rave for over an hour and she was only really pacified when he pressed £100 into her unresisting hands. He promised her faithfully that he would vet all his guests more carefully in future.

'You'd damn well better,' said Galadriel. 'But don't even think about sending me any more until the weekend after next. My nerves are shot, and I need a break. I'm going to a retreat.'

In fact, she was going to stay with her sister, Patricia, in Worthing. Married to a retired railway clerk, Patricia was as normal as roast beef on Sunday, which was exactly what Galadriel needed right now. Tamika had agreed to take care of things for a couple of weeks, during which Galadriel Starchild would revert to Doreen Mudd. If that wasn't a retreat, she was buggered if she knew what was!

# A Glastonbury Tale

*Chapter 9*

As September wandered to an end, Alan Smart grew impatient with Geoff Bendix. The £20,000 the former had loaned the latter six months ago was now worth £30,000. Mr Smart didn't mind people owing him money—it was what made his world go 'round—but they had to pay their instalments on time. Oh, violence could be fun, but when it came right down to it, he'd rather have the cash. Therefore, his phone call to Geoff was firm but fair, in his mind at least.

To Geoff, it was extremely threatening. And, to make matters worse, he received a letter from his bank by registered post the same morning suggesting he might like to call in and discuss his financial situation. Until he did, in fact, no future cheques would be honoured. Shit, he thought, there were a couple still floating about, and one of them was to the golf club renewing his subscription. He phoned his 'chum' Nigel, the bank manager. The call was not received with as much friendliness as in days of yore, but at least it was received. However, the news was not good. Unless Geoff could square the circle, he was in real trouble.

'What if I offer more collateral against another loan? Consolidate the debts, put everything on a new footing?' he asked.

Nigel pointed out the bank already had it all. All three of his houses and both his businesses. Geoff sat up straight at his desk, the phone clenched in his hand, his sphincter clenched in fear.

'Nigel, old mate' he said, trying hard to sound confident. 'This is just a temporary embarrassment. I've a big one ready to land. Within a week. Three at the outside. Property sale in London, ex-council house. I'll make at least forty thou profit on it. Just waiting on the solicitors, you know how it is.'

'Got the deeds, Geoff? Letters of exchange and all that boring stuff? Can't even begin to discuss it without those,' said Nigel.

'Of course, no problem, been meaning to drop by and sort things out, but what with going to and from London to clinch this sale, I've been a bit rushed.'

'Well, stop in with the paperwork next week and we can have a talk. Let's say Tuesday at two pm, how's that? Otherwise, you're in danger of going tits up, I'm afraid.'

'How about the cheques I've got outstanding?' pleaded Geoff. 'One's to the golf club. It'd be a bit embarrassing if that bounced.'

'Yeah, all right' said Nigel wearily, 'but no more. And come see me with something I can show the auditors next Tuesday. Don't forget, okay?'

Geoff was trembling when he put down the phone. Three days. Just three fucking days to sort the bank and pay Mr Smart £1000. Why the hell did he bullshit about his father's house? That was stupid. Head in hands, he tried desperately to think of a plan. The first of the month would bring a whole slew of new final demands and threats of court action. He could almost hear the tread of the bailiff's boots.

Not for the first time, he thought of the scrapyard. There were two- and a-bit acres of land and was on a junction between a small lane and a larger one connecting to the main road into Glastonbury. The site would be worth real money if it could be built on; enough to pay off Smart, his credit cards, and even that tosser Nigel. But until he could get planning permission, there was sweet f-a he could do with it. The bank already held the deeds of his other assets, including the three squalid houses he was letting out. They were mortgaged well beyond their worth anyway, thanks to a dodgy pal who had taken his commission and run. His Range Rover was leased, and he owed money on that as well. The small house he lived in was rented. Maybe he could loot the Grey Havens account? But there probably wasn't much there as he hadn't paid anything into it for weeks.

Geoff made an attempt to prioritise. What was the worst threat? Mr Smart, by far. The bank could wind you up, but Smart could—and would— quite literally, chop you up. On the other hand, Smart was also businessman who loved a deal. Might he take the scrapyard in full and final settlement of the debt? Possibly, but there would be a risk in even offering it: he would know Geoff had finally run out money.

What if he really could get the deed to his father's house? That would be easier to sell than the scrapyard and would actually make the bundle he had told Nigel it would. He could forge the old bugger's signature and start the ball rolling, put it up for sale at a silly price. But that wouldn't get him the thousand he needed immediately. Cash was king and right now he was a bloody serf without a penny to his name.

Time to make a plan. No use running around like a headless

chicken. First things first. Try to get hold of the deeds for both the house and the scrapyard. But where were the buggers?

He drove to his office and parked a street away so his landlord wouldn't see the car. Tina was off today (just as well, he owed her money, too) so he let himself in, almost tripping over a pile of mail just inside the door. He hoped the documents he wanted would be in one of the filing cabinets. They weren't. He went through his desk, Tina's desk, and everywhere else, including the cloakroom. Nothing. Lots of papers, stacks of files, but not the one holding the stiff legal papers he so desperately sought. Panic reigned. Then it poured.

Geoff sat at his desk and tried to think. As a sort of displacement therapy, he picked up the mail and went through it. He tossed aside all envelopes with windows or utility company logos, which left only three. Two were advertisements. The third was addressed to 'Havens Holdings' and contained a cheque for five hundred lovely, wonderful, English pounds. A note accompanying the cheque stated that the writer, Mr Tiptree, was sorry if he had caused any inconvenience when he changed banks a couple of months ago and forgot to reinstate the standing order for his rent.

Oh, fucking joy! Five hundred quid! Not enough to get him out of trouble, but fully half. Perhaps it would even hold Mr Smart off for a week or two. No title deeds, though. There was only one place they could be now and that was in a small brown suitcase on top of his father's wardrobe. Geoff vaguely remembered seeing it somewhere in his father's rooms. He knew that was where the old bugger kept anything he thought important enough not to throw away. The more he picked the scab of memory, the more confident he became that if the deeds were anywhere, they were in that case. That meant a trip to Galadriel's. With a bit of luck, he might even be able to con her out of a few pounds. With hope now burning in his flabby breast, Geoff Bendix went forth.

~~~

Mail had arrived at Grey Havens that morning, too. The usual rubbish advertising plus two envelopes with stars and mystic symbols on for Mrs Spottiswood, and a very terse communication from the electricity company requiring immediate payment of an outstanding bill. Galadriel wasn't due back for a few days more. She had left the cheque book, but Tamika couldn't sign the cheques so even if she drove into town there was bugger all she could do. The bill was for £457. She could phone and say the owner was away, ask if they would hold off for a day or two, but doubted that would cut much ice. Probably the only thing that would be cut would be the power, and Tamika could only imagine the ruck that would cause amongst the residents. She was considering paying the bill herself and getting the money back from Galadriel later when in breezed Geoff Bendix. Tamika explained that Galadriel was visiting a relative and wouldn't be back until later in the week.

'That's a bugger' said Geoff. 'Anyway, where's the paying-in book for the Grey Havens account?'

When this account had been set up, Galadriel had insisted on using an 'ethical' bank. Geoff had eventually given in after endless lectures about most High Street banks and their unsavoury practices. So, it was the Co-op Bank that got the Havens account, which saved it from joining Geoff's other businesses in their incestuous fiscal morass. Tamika didn't like

Geoff and didn't trust him, but she couldn't see what damage he could do with the paying-in book. She showed him the final demand from the electricity company.

'No, no,' he said, 'they got their wires crossed. Get it? Wires crossed!'

Tamika didn't even smile.

'Paid it day before yesterday. Just hasn't gone through.' He took the letter and said he would sort it, no worries.

Doris came in and announced the hoover was blocked again. Tamika looked at Geoff and said, 'Lucky you're here, then, isn't it?'

'Not in this jacket' he growled. 'I'll get Desmond in, all right?'

Tamika didn't bother to reply. The man was a waste of a good skin. She got up and followed Doris. She'd unblock the bloody thing herself.

When she was out of the room, Geoff quickly took a couple of cheques from the middle of the Grey Haven's cheque book and slipped them into his pocket along with the paying-in book. He'd have no trouble forging Galadriel's signature; it was already on a pile of stuff she knew nothing about. Finding the petty cash tin open but empty, he left the office and went upstairs to his father's room. The door was unlocked, he eased it open and peered inside.

Bert was lying on his big sofa, dozing, the remains of his breakfast on a small table beside him. Geoff crept past him into the bedroom where he found an unmade bed, a huge chest of drawers, and a large 1950s wardrobe with a pile of suitcases on top. A small brown one was uppermost. Geoff was not a tall man and the case was just beyond his reach.

Looking around, he saw a walking stick with a curved

handle leaning by the bed. He used this to try to hook the top case without disturbing the others, all the while straining his ears to catch any sound from the next room. As he stretched up as high as he could in the hot, airless bedroom, gravity lent a hand, but with more gusto than Geoff could have wished. The top three cases tumbled down onto his head with a crash. None of them was particularly heavy, but all were dusty. Geoff sneezed. When he opened his eyes, his father was standing in the doorway. His body had been diminished by time, but his voice was as strong as ever.

'What the FUCK!'

Instantly, Geoff was a child again, up to no good, snooping and prying where he had no business to be. And suddenly it wasn't a frail old man in pyjamas standing there anymore, it was an angry giant, broad leather belt in hand, ready to dispense terrifying and painful justice.

Picking up one of the larger cases from the floor, Geoff threw it at Bert, knocking him over. He moved quickly, the small brown suitcase clutched to his chest, but just as he exited the bedroom, Bert's foot hooked over his ankle, causing him to crash to the floor, his face landing in the remains of the old man's breakfast. He still had the case, though, and scrambled to his feet, bits of bacon, fried egg, and tomato ketchup now clinging to the side of his head.

Moving fast, desperate to escape, Geoff headed for the door and collided with Tamika, who had come up to see what all the noise was about. The force of the impact caused her head to hit the doorframe and she collapsed on the landing, stunned.

Mrs Spottiswood ran out from her room to find out what the hell was going on and Geoff, attempting to regain his balance, stumbled against her ample bosom and quickly became entangled in the numerous bead necklaces and talismans there. Mrs Spottiswood was devoted to peace, harmony, and celestial rhythms, but the slap she delivered to the side of Geoff's head indicated she could cope with discord, too, if necessary.

His head ringing, Geoff stumbled down the stairs and into the hall. There he met Doris, who by this time had gathered enough information from all the shouting to know how to proceed. Having grown up with a herd of brothers, she knew just where to aim the business end of the vacuum cleaner on its long metal tube. With a powerful lunge, she swung for his balls. Geoff bent double in agony, somehow managed to stagger to his car. That was when he realized the little brown case had parted from its handle at some point in the proceedings. He threw the handle into the back seat and at last made his escape.

He consoled himself with the fact that at least he had a cheque for five big ones, plus the two blank cheques and the paying-in book. Parking up by his office, he went in and cleaned up as much as he could. Then he wrote a cheque payable to 'cash' for £700. He doubted there would be more than that available, even with the £500 he was paying in. At the bank, the cashier had a quiet word with the undermanager (the smears of ketchup around Geoff's ear gave her cause for concern), but eventually did pay out.

With money in hand, Geoff went home and considered his next move. Seven hundred . . . well, say six hundred, that should keep Smart off his back for a week at least. The deeds, though. How he'd get his hands on those was anybody's guess. And once Galadriel got back and discovered he'd cleaned out her bank account, she certainly wouldn't help him. Oh well, fuck it, he'd drift on to the golf club for an hour or two, have a drink, and get his breath back.

~~~

The only resident of Grey Havens to witness Geoff's departure was Granny Toogood. She'd been keeping a low profile since the incident with the snake and was lurking in some bushes near the house. She didn't know what to make of his speeding off like that, but hoped it meant trouble for someone. She returned to her lurking and crept closer to the garden that had once been her private domain. Miss Browne had inspired some of the residents to get involved in her plans and they were now clearing the flowerbeds. Granny's aconite had been discovered.

'It really is an exceedingly dangerous plant,' Miss Browne was saying. 'You'll notice I'm wearing gloves to protect my hands from its effects. A surprising number of houseplants can be toxic, too, especially to cats. If you're interested in knowing more, the local gardening club have asked me to give a talk about them. It used to be one of my specialities back in the day because so many medicinal herbs can be quite dangerous if not handled correctly.'

Granny made a mental note to find out when the talk was. She still had a slight feeling of unease about Miss Browne, but she might as well take advantage of her knowledge, especially with all these houseplants filling every available space. When it came to the destruction of Bast, she'd bite through cast iron to kill the bastard.

At the club, everyone who knew Geoff avoided him. The smell of impending bankruptcy hung around him like dog shit on his shoe. He drank alone and paid for his drinks in cash.

The protocol for making his payments to Mr Smart wasn't complicated. He had to drive to a certain garage on the Meare Road about five miles out of town and place the cash in the hands of a man-mountain in the workshop there. This giant then counted the money and handed over a raffle ticket as a receipt. It was the sort of raffle ticket used at church bazars and jolly fundraising events throughout the land, though in this particular raffle the prize was keeping out of hospital for another month. The deadline was midnight, unless a prior arrangement had been made, which of course cost extra. Geoff had no arrangement today. He'd used that option last month.

It was raining when he climbed into his large, white Range Rover. There wasn't another one like it in Glastonbury, a fact that had pleased him no end once upon a time. Now, not so much. He drove the long and lonely road out of town, the pouring rain and the flat, grey landscape only adding to his gloom. Geoff's anxiety increased as he neared his destination and all too soon he could see the garage ahead. The pumps stood under a neon canopy, the light flickering down on oily, rain-slicked cement. A red door bearing a 'PAY HERE' sign stood between two windows so obscured by grime and fly-blown advertisements that the light from within barely showed. The big sliding doors that led into the workshop were shut. No one appeared to be about, but that wasn't unusual.

Geoff parked next to the pumps and went into the shop. The usual procedure was to nod to whoever was behind the counter then walk through another door into the oily cavern of the garage. As he eased past the small counter, he noticed the till was open. That was odd. Inside the garage, a dim bulb hanging from the ceiling provided enough light for Geoff to see that the man-mountain was in residence but wouldn't be issuing any raffle tickets today. Or ever again if the amount of blood and grey matter surrounding what was left of his head was anything to go by. One bloodshot eye stared out of the gory mess and looked accusingly at Geoff, who nearly passed out. Blood was all over the floor and Geoff saw he'd trodden in it. He was holding onto the door frame to stop from falling over and realized he'd probably touched the counter, the outer door, everything, in fact. Using the cuff of his jacket he tried to erase his prints, but only managed to transfer greasy smudges from the woodwork onto his sleeve. Backing out slowing, cringing every time his jacket brushed against anything, he made his escape.

This was Geoff's second exit from an unpleasant situation that day, and this one, too, was witnessed. As he climbed into his big, white, easily recognizable vehicle, a small, nondescript one drove up and stopped at the pumps. Geoff didn't hang around. He sped off into the darkness, a very frightened man. He would have been downright terrified had he known that, after the police had been summoned and received the witness's description of his Range Rover, one cop stepped out of the whirl of flashing blue lights to make a discreet phone call.

The recipient of the call, Mr Robert Smart, thanked the officer and said there would be a not inconsiderable bonus if all further intelligence regarding this dreadful crime were passed on to him in a timely manner as form and custom required. Then he hung up and began to plan discreet, careful, and above all painful vengeance. As sure as the rain fell on that remote garage, Mr Smart's wrath would fall on Geoff Bendix, guilty or not.

*Chapter 10*

A silence had descended on Grey Havens after Geoff had gone. As is common after a battle, those left standing looked around to see who else had survived. Tamika got shakily to her feet. Putting her hand to the back of her head, she felt a bump the size of a pigeon's egg, but determined she was otherwise unhurt. Bert had made it onto the sofa and appeared to be okay, though based on the amount of cursing going on, he was very angry.

Doris made Bert and Tamika some good strong tea with lots of sugar. Mrs Spottiswood was all for calling the police, but Bert thought not, and Tamika agreed with him. Geoff hadn't actually stolen anything. The paying-in book was as much his property as anyone's. Yes, she and Bert had been knocked about, but no serious damage had been done. Not enough to bother the police with, anyway.

As soon as they were left alone they opened the small brown case and went through its contents. There appeared to be nothing there but dusty old documents, however, so they decided whatever Geoff had been looking for must not have been in there after all.

~~~

On Wednesday morning, Doris and Tamika were having a quiet cup of coffee in the kitchen. Everything seemed to be back to normal, and there had been a phone call from Galadriel saying she would return the following day.

The front doorbell rang. Tamika answered it and there was Paddy Doyle. He looked serious and asked if they could talk, so she took him into the office and closed the door.

'What's wrong?' she asked.

'Nothing to worry you,' he said, 'but when was the last time you saw Geoff Bendix?'

'Geoff Bendix! As a matter of fact, I saw him yesterday.' Tamika told him what had happened.

'Are you all right?' he asked, his face serious and concerned.

'I'm fine, it was just a bump.'

'May I?' he asked and reached out and very gently stroked the back of her head. 'How's your vision? Seeing okay? No double vision, headaches, or the like?'

'I'm fine,' said Tamika.

Doyle leaned back again and asked her how well she knew Geoff Bendix.

'Well enough to dislike him. He's allegedly financing this place, but the bills are never paid on time and he's always pleading poverty.'

'Is there any kind of emotional relationship between Geoff and Galadriel?'

'No, I'm pretty sure there isn't. I don't know what they were like when the arrangement was set up, but I don't believe there's anything going on now. Why are you asking these questions? Is Geoff in trouble?'

Doyle told her about what had been found in the Meare

Road garage and how Geoff's car had been seen driving away. 'We've got forensics going all over the scene but whether Geoff Bendix was the perpetrator or not, we don't yet know. We haven't been able to locate him. Do you think his father would know where he is? I know he doesn't like the police, but would he speak to me, do you think?'

'Let's find out' said Tamika and took Doyle up to the old man's room.

The interview went better than Tamika had feared. Doyle introduced himself and told Bert his son's car had been seen leaving the scene of a murder and that the victim was a known associate of a loan shark.

'Loan shark, eh? That doesn't surprise me,' said Bert. He told Doyle about his son's gambling habit and all the money he'd given him over the years. 'Always said he just needed a loan to get some damned scheme or other up and running, then he'd make a fortune and pay me back. So, I helped him out. Had no choice, really. I wasn't well and he was on my fucking back all the time.'

'Has he ever paid back any of the money?' asked Tamika.

Bert shook his head. 'Dribs and drabs,' he said. Then, turning to Doyle he continued, 'He's a bloody fool, always was, but I don't think he's a killer. Hasn't got the bottle for it.'

'Not even if he were threatened?' said Doyle.

'Nah. He'd do a runner before he'd fight back.'

Doyle thought about that. It tallied with other things he had heard about the man. He asked Bert if he knew where his son might run to, but the old man had no idea. Doyle asked if he could see the suitcase or whatever it was Geoff had tried to take.

Bert pointed to the table on which he and Tamika had spread the contents of the case. 'It's just a lot of old papers. Insurance policies and all that kind of rubbish' said Bert. 'I don't know why he'd be so ruddy keen to get his hands on any of that.'

'Could he have hidden something in here without you knowing it, Mr Bendix?' asked Doyle as he glanced through the pile.

'Could have,' said Bert, 'but why?'

There was no answer to that and as it obviously had nothing to do with the murder he was investigating, Doyle thanked Bert for seeing him and got up to leave. Tamika went with him to the front door and watched as he drove away. Then she sighed and went back up to Bert's room. There had been something in that collection of documents that had caught her eye.

~~~

Doyle's next stop was Geoff's scrapyard. The big metal gates were open and a small, beat up van with 'Bendix Builders' written on the side was parked up near the entrance to a large brick building. He considered radioing for uniform backup but knowing what he did about Geoff Bendix decided it would be unnecessary. Walking up to the doors, which took up almost the whole front of the building, he looked inside. There were benches all around the walls and a few pieces of machinery. Pillar drills and the like. Engines, gear boxes, and piles of domestic junk were grouped in clusters on the cement floor. The one area that appeared to be in current use was a bench against the wall near the door, which had a few tools on a rack above it. In front of the bench was an eviscerated dishwasher, its component parts spread around it as if it had been attacked by a very methodical predator. A young man in tatty dungarees, dreadlocks, and bare feet was currently working away inside it, oblivious to all else.

Doyle walked over, held up his warrant card, and said 'Detective Sergeant Doyle. And you are?' Doyle always went in friendly; he could do it the other way, but much preferred friendly. The result was often so much better for all concerned.

Desmond looked up, not at all fazed by this big bloke flashing a card at him and asking who he was. He stood up, wiped his hands on a grubby bit of rag, and told him.

'Desmond Clarke. I work for Geoff Bendix. How can I help you?'

'You can tell me when you last saw Mr Bendix.'

Desmond didn't ask why. People were always looking for Geoff these days and at least this one was legit and polite.

'Couple days ago. I haven't been paid for two weeks and came in to see if he was about. He wasn't, so I hung around trying to fix up this clapped out dishwasher for a friend.'

'Mind if I take a look around?'

'No problem.'

Doyle let Desmond show him the site. It was a typical scrapyard and there were no surprises until they came upon Geoff's white Range Rover parked up at the back, tucked away behind an old bus. It had been driven in with some force and was so close to a huge, overgrown hedge that only the passenger door was accessible. There was nobody inside and the vehicle was locked.

Doyle radioed for SOCO. He believed Desmond when he said he had no idea how long it had been there.

'Anything missing that you know of? Car, van, motorbike, anything drivable?' he asked.

They did a careful walk around and up and down the alleys of dead vehicles while Desmond tried to determine if anything was gone. Then he noticed a lighter patch of grass in front of a pile of tyres.

'There was a small Ford parked here. It was a runner that had failed its MOT. I remember because I was thinking of getting it for my mum, but Lionel, he's the mechanic, told me the steering was shot, so I didn't.'

'Do you know where the documentation is kept? Logbooks and the like?' asked Doyle.

Desmond led him back into the garage. Doyle was about to walk across what he thought was just another bit of grimy floor when the young man shouted at him to stop.

'Hang on' he shouted, 'you don't want to step on that'.

'That' turned out to be a piece of thin plywood covering the inspection pit. Desmond came over and kicked the plywood aside. It was like the letter box to Hades Doyle thought as he peered into the dark depths. A filthy concrete slot about four feet wide and God knows how deep. An oily, fetid, smell emanated from it.

'The fitters wanted an inspection pit, said Desmond, 'so Geoff moaned and groaned, finally gave in and said he'd get it done'. Of course, being Geoff, it was never straight forward. As well as a pit for the mechanics, he wanted a little hidey hole for his hooky gear didn't he.' 'So, he had it dug deeper and a false floor put in' 'Of course, bloody thing filled with water so it had to be pumped out before you could get in'. 'In the end no one bothered, it stinks to high heaven and God knows what is at the bottom now, it's full of junk, I know that'. 'The plywood might take your weight and then again it might not,' he added with a chuckle as he kicked the cover back in place, where once again it blended into the dirty concrete floor. 'There used to be a traffic cone on it, but someone used it for something else and didn't put it back. We all know it's there, so we just automatically walk around it.' And with that he led Doyle into the office.

In the office, Doyle was shown a filing cabinet in which there were piles of tax discs, logbooks, MOT certificates, and a few very old, very grubby girly magazines. He and Desmond went through all the documents. There was a dozen or more for Ford cars of all sorts, but none looked recent. Another drawer held hundreds of ignition keys, some with fobs, others in bundles held together with rusty wire. Finally, with a bit of prompting, Desmond remembered the missing car was a Ford Fiesta, and it was white. He remembered that because his mum liked white cars. They showed up better at night.

Now Doyle had something to go on. It wasn't much, but it was more than he'd had when he set out that morning. He chatted to Desmond until the SOCO unit arrived. No Sally this time, just some surly bloke who looked at the Range Rover, sucked his teeth, and said he'd have to get a low-loader, as if this were somehow Doyle's fault. Doyle made a note of Desmond's home address and suggested he drop by the nick at his earliest convenience to make an official statement.

By the time Doyle was back in the nick himself, Mr Smart had been brought up to date. His connection with the dead man was now known to the police, and the police were actively seeking Geoff Bendix. Thus, whether or not Geoff had brained Big Willy and stolen his takings was almost beside the point;

he had to be found and neutralised before he could talk to the police.

Robert Smart opened a drawer, selected a burner phone from the top of the pile, and called a man whose services he used when he needed some distance between himself and his victims. Leonard Crabbe was not cheap, but then ruthless psychopaths who successfully run discreet debt recovery services never are. Crabbe was no muscle-bound thug, but he was devious, relentless, and specialised in witness protection. He protected witnesses so carefully the only person they ever spoke to again was Saint Peter.

~~~

The subject of these preparations was a long way away, driving a clapped-out Ford Fiesta. After collecting the car, he had made a brief visit to his home for clothes and toiletries, and to his office for his laptop and accounts books. Anything, in fact, that might be of use to any official (or unofficial) receiver. Geoff Bendix, as his father had predicted, was doing a runner.

~~~

During the course of her stay with her sister, Galadriel had discovered that 'dull' could actually be good for one's wellbeing and spiritual harmony. As could scones, cakes, and buns made with highly processed white flour instead of a gravelly artisan mixture that broke your teeth. She arrived back at Grey Havens on Thursday, full of the joy of a beautiful autumn morning.

It didn't last long. The house itself was spotless and smelled of furniture polish, and Tamika had the coffee on the go as soon as she arrived, but the phone had been cut off and there was a pile of letters all demanding action on the payment of bills both ancient and modern. They pertained to water rates, house insurance, oil for the central heating, and electricity, amongst other things. Tamika had worked out how much money was needed to pay for everything, and it came to just over £2500. Galadriel put her head in her hands and all the spiritual harmony and good vibes she had brought back with her went out the celestial window.

Then Tamika told her about Geoff's visit and what Doyle had said about Geoff's current troubles, so there was no point in trying to contact him. Galadriel had no idea how much money, if any, she had in the bank, nor could she phone them to find out. All she had was the remains of the cash Dai had given her, which probably wouldn't even buy groceries for the week.

Galadriel was getting ready to go into town and speak to the bank when Dai drove in. Word had reached him that Geoff Bendix was a wanted man and, knowing of his involvement with Grey Havens, Dai guessed there would be trouble brewing. He had been putting a lot of thought into the ancient well and had decided this would be the perfect time to share his ideas with Galadriel.

Galadriel's mood lightened at the sight of his bearded face. She asked Tamika to bring them some coffee in the office and led Dai away. By the time Tamika came in with the cups, they were sitting side by side at the desk going through bank statements. Dai was saying he'd heard Geoff was on the run not just from the police but also a right nasty bastard he owed money to.

'Forget rocks and hard places,' he said, 'the stupid sod's between jail and someone who'll have his balls off if he doesn't pay up.'

Then, seeing she wasn't wanted, Tamika went upstairs to tell Bert what was going on.

~~~

As it happened, Geoff Bendix was being missed by all sorts of people that day. Currently he was being missed by his sort-of secretary, Tina, who had opened the office to find the safe both open and empty. Her gaze fell on the big leather chair behind his desk. A chair she and Geoff had found so useful in the sexual gymnastics that were the real reason he employed her. He was two weeks late with her wages and she was three weeks late with her period. And that bastard was responsible for both of these facts.

Tina's day was not improved when a knock on the door revealed the unpleasant presence of Leonard Crabbe. She was used to all sorts of men coming into Geoff's office. Some undressed her with their eyes, some tried it on in less subtle ways, and a few were really there for business. She could tell this man was really there for business. He showed her a card that had 'Court Bailiff' written on it and he had a pile of paper in a clipboard, but he smelled bent. Bent and dangerous, so she gave him all the information he asked for without hesitation, including Geoff's home address and the address of the scrapyard. It had been four days since she had last seen him. The only family she knew of was a father who lived somewhere in an old people's home in Glastonbury, but they didn't get on. Crabbe's small dark eyes stared at her without blinking and he made little mewing sounds and tiny grunts as he wrote down her answers. Then he simply got up and left. She suddenly felt the air was a lot cleaner and before anyone else could turn up, locked the office and went home.

Crabbe followed her, of course, and made note of her address. The old folks' home he would look into later. Using one of the few red telephone boxes still around, he reported back to his principal. Crabbe never carried a mobile. He didn't trust them. He was of the old school and believed in the old ways. Much, for example, could be accomplished with a burning cigarette end, and such equipment was easy to carry without arousing suspicion.

His next stop was the scrapyard, just to be sure the subject wasn't hiding out there. He didn't think he would be, but it paid to be sure. As he drove in, he saw a van parked near the open doors of a large, brick building. From inside he could hear the sound of banging. Entering the dark and dusty interior, he saw a young man struggling to reassemble a dishwasher. The radio was blaring out some noise Mr Crabbe found annoying, so he unplugged it.

Desmond turned around to see what had happened to his music. Seeing the small, still figure of Mr Crabbe made him jump and drop the hammer he had in his hand, which, though he didn't know it, actually increased his personal safety. He was treated to the same card Tina had been shown and, being a friendly young man and innocent of the ways of the world, dusted off a chair and offered his visitor coffee and as much information as he wanted. Desmond's answers were similar to Tina's but included Geoff's involvement in Grey Havens and the fact that his father lived there. He confirmed there was no love lost in that relationship. This removed one lever Crabbe had been considering, but a question mark hung over the woman called Galadriel.

~~~

While the relentless Mr Crabbe prospected for information, Dai Griffiths reviewed all that he had acquired so far. He had literally taken Galadriel by the hand and visited her bank. They had informed her that she had just over £800 in her account, thanks to some rents being paid by standing order on the first of the month. Galadriel left most of the chores that involved money to Tamika, but even she could see there should have been a lot more than that. Tamika had long suspected Geoff had been hiving off rents by having some paid into his other accounts, but Galadriel had never listened to her. She listened to Dai, though. He paid for the telephone to be connected, using a credit card so it would be back on quickly. Then he took her to a little pub outside of town and described his 'rescue package' to her over a vegetarian cutlet and a couple of bottles of free-range wine.

When they returned to Grey Havens in the late afternoon, all was sweetness and light. Dai drove off smiling and Galadriel went to her caravan. Tomorrow she was going to move into the no-longer-spare apartment. Tamika wasn't given any details, just assured that all would be well, the harmonies were good, and not to worry. She suspected this was right up there with the captain of the *Titanic* telling the fiddle player not to worry because he had a wooden instrument and wood floats.

Later, going into the office to retrieve the coffee cups, she saw a pile of scribbled notes and drawings on Galadriel's desk. One of the drawings turned out to be a plan of the house. Lines had been put through a number of rooms. Bert's and

Mr Tiptree's on the first floor, and Carmel's and Major Dennis's on the second. There was a question mark against Granny Toogood's on the top floor. Doodles and words written on the margins mapped the course of the discussion that had taken place. A little box with a sort of halo over it apparently represented Grey Havens. Pilgrims were mentioned, and there was a small sketch of a well with an egg cup above it. 'No, wait, this is Glastonbury, thought Tamika. That must be a chalice.

So, that was the plan. Turf out some residents and turn the place into what? A psychic guest house, a Tantric B&B, or just somewhere for Dai to park his sheep so he could fleece them even more? And the well? What was that all about? Galadriel must have told Dai what young Desmond had said about the site. No wonder he had looked like the cat that had got the cream when he drove away. But developing that site would take real money. Did Dai have that sort of capital? No, he would probably have to borrow it, and the most obvious collateral was Grey Havens itself. Would Galadriel be that daft? Possibly. Probably, in fact. After all, she'd fallen for Geoff's plan. But you'd have thought she'd have learned her lesson.

Tamika sat down and seriously considered the situation. She liked working at Grey Havens. It suited her. And it was a good business. It needed more cash put it into it, but it was basically sound. The only weak link had been Geoff Bendix and now he was out of the picture. Trouble was, that left a hole in the finances. A hole Galadriel couldn't fill on her own. Tamika went up to see Bert. When she left his room later that evening, she was carrying the small brown suitcase, now full of highly organised papers.

A Glastonbury Tale

*Chapter 11*

Mr Smart was in his place of work. It smelled of pigs. He didn't like pigs, or any livestock come to that. He wasn't into rural. But he was into the efficient disposal of waste, hence his ownership of this modest farm on the Somerset levels. The screams had stopped now. Shame that, they indicated the subject was getting the point. Or the blow torch, or the pliers, or the bolt cutters. Or even a bit of electricity. All tools in the trade of someone who was serious about getting every last drop of information. He now knew who had robbed and killed Big Willie, where the money was, and that the man was very, very sorry. Now there was just the loose end of Geoff Bendix to tie up.

What had once been human (but was now pig food) was winched down from the ceiling of the barn. It was a special barn. Not big, but completely soundproof. Robert Smart shed his disposable apron, took off his rubber boots, and went into the farmhouse for his breakfast. He was always hungry after a little session like this. Devilled kidneys, just the thing, but they had to be fresh. These were.

~~~

Breakfast at Grey Havens featured wholesome granola as gritty as a freshly laid road, solid ingots of artisan-made brown bread, salt-free butter, and low-sugar preserves. Galadriel, remembering the breakfasts at her sister's house, gazed longingly at the stodgy, unhealthful white bread Doris was toasting for Bert.

Tamika had called in sick, so Galadriel was going through the post herself. A registered letter had come from some solicitors in Eastbourne called Calthrop and Peabody. It was written in the finest legalese money could buy and represented the first salvo in a barrage threatening Galadriel with legal action in regard to the sudden death of the claimant's sister, Mrs Irene Meldrum. Almost hidden amongst the weasel words was a request for the writer to be furnished with the names of Galadriel's insurance company and solicitor. Geoff had bought the insurance from a dodgy mate of his (and probably hadn't kept up the payments), and Galadriel didn't have a solicitor. She phoned her Welsh wizard; surely, he would know what to do.

'Look here, my girl, there's nothing whatever for you to worry about,' he said. 'I have just the man for the job, known him years and years, clever fellow and a very good lawyer. Name of Ethan Bedlow. I've got an appointment with him on Monday, so just you come along and I've no doubt he'll be able to ease your mind.'

In fact, Ethan Bedlow was already an accepted backer for the new Grey Havens Pilgrims Rest and Healing Well Company Limited. Bringing Galadriel along on Monday would be an opportunity for her to meet Ethan in the guise of knight in shining armour rather than a smooth operator looking for an investment opportunity.

~~~

In the common room, a small, hand-written note had appeared on the residents' notice board. Miss Browne's talk on poisonous houseplants was scheduled for 12th October at The Friends Meeting House. Granny established that both Mrs Spottiswood and Major Dennis were planning to go and asked if she could travel with them. 'Safety in numbers,' she thought. 'I don't want to be the only resident attending.' She also offered to help Miss Browne with her horticultural endeavours, thinking this might give her access to plants of particular interest. Unfortunately, her offer was misunderstood, and she was allocated a cleared section of the vegetable patch in which, together with Carmel, she was instructed to plant a row of leeks and broad beans for over-wintering. This took longer than it should have done and tried Granny's patience sorely because Carmel kept stopping to check the phases of the moon and adjust the alignment of the rows accordingly.

~~~

Geoff Bendix, now in darkest Cornwall, was driving on what was laughingly called an 'A' road, when he noticed a tatty, hand-drawn sign attached to a gate: CARAVANS TO RENT. In the corner of a derelict pasture, a few old caravans were slowly decaying into the landscape. The house was a stone building typical in that part of the world, with small, dirt-encrusted windows that faced the road. This was not chocolate-box Cornwall, nor did it feature in any tourist guide. Geoff parked up in the yard and, after a brief negotiation with a monosyllabic son of the soil, was allotted a caravan. It had running water, a chemical loo, and occasional electricity. He could hide his car in what remained of a large barn, swap number plates at some point, and keep his head down. It would do for now.

~~~

Tamika hadn't felt a single pang of guilt when she'd called in sick on Friday morning and headed to Bristol to visit Dr Sebastian Grove, a favourite lecturer of hers. His speciality was land law and commercial investments. He had been her tutor, mentor, and eventually a friend. They drank tea in his study while she gave him an overview of the situation, after which she placed all the papers she had got from Bert on his desk. These included insurance policies, hire purchase agreements, and similar detritus accumulated by an old man who never threw an 'official' document away. But Tamika had attended business college and she knew title deeds when she saw them, as well as company registration documents.

'This is a title deed for a parcel of land of approximately two and a quarter acres at the junction of Basket Maker's Lane and Gypsy Lane, Glastonbury. Stapled to this was another document that appeared to be the articles of association for a limited company called Bendix Land & Gravel. I've not had time to do any search in Companies House or the land registry, but they look right to me.'

'And these are in the name of Bertram Stanley Bendix, with an address in London,' said Dr Grove. He leaned forward and peered closely at them. 'Dated two years ago. What does your friend Bert make of that?'

'That was around the time his son moved him into Grey Havens. Bert was so sick with pneumonia he barely remembers it. He was on a lot of medication and hardly conscious most of the time. He thinks his son also took one of his bank books away then. At least, he didn't have it anymore when he finally recovered. And based on my knowledge of his son, it wouldn't surprise me at all. In fact, I wouldn't mind betting Geoff Bendix wanted an asset his bank couldn't get hold of, and of course, he could boomerang any rent between companies.'

'Then there is a title deed for an ex-council house in Bert's name' said Dr Grove. 'Has that been assigned to the son?'

'No, and Bert has no record of any rents accruing from it. And look at this,' Tamika added, passing over a document with 'Last Will and Testament' in ornate lettering across the top.

Dr Grove examined it. 'Standard stuff' he said. 'Also dated a couple of years ago and leaving everything to his only heir, Geoffrey Bendix.'

'Yes,' said Tamika, 'but that's not Bert's signature. He says he never signed it. He was pressured to, but he told his son to sod off.'

'Hardly a legal term' said Dr Grove smiling, 'but I think I get the gentleman's drift. Okay, you have a fraud, but it won't be easy to scotch this will, so get him to make another.'

'That's one of the things I wanted to talk to you about. Bert says he has no one to leave anything to, certainly not his son. So, he wants me to get the lot if I promise to look after him until he dies.'

'If you're willing to do that, there's no legal reason for you not to inherit. I dare say you will find the son has embezzled money from the father, so if he did contest the will he'd be on dodgy ground. You can act as executor of course, but I wouldn't try to get power of attorney. That might prove difficult.'

'Okay. And here's the other thing. His son is on the run from his creditors and is probably going to end up being bankrupt. He had money in Grey Havens and, with him gone, the owner, Galadriel, is being courted by a dodgy bloke who has his eye on the house for his own purposes, which include turfing out some of the residents and letting the apartments as a sort of mystic holiday home. And Bert will be one of the first to go, and I expect he won't want me about, either. So, I'm thinking of making Galadriel an offer of a partnership using the money from the sale of Bert's house or the scrapyard. Or maybe forming a limited company to run Grey Havens as a proper business.'

Dr Grove's advice was to get all the information, land registry and everything, first. 'Well, not quite first' he said. 'Get Bert to write a new will sooner rather than later. Realise what assets you can and set up a joint bank account and simple partnership agreement to cover the legal requirements. I can recommend a good solicitor to advise you if that would help.'

They talked a while longer, then Tamika got up to leave. There was a pause. Finally, Dr Grove said, 'You're a bright person. You were one of my best students. Are you sure you want to settle for running a home for old hippies?'

'It does sound odd, doesn't it? But I like it. It's more challenging than you might think. And if I had more say in the business and was able to afford some essential repairs, I'm sure it would be successful. Oh, and there's a magic well in the garden. What more could a girl want?'

~~~

On Sunday, Paddy Doyle was listening to any little bird (or rat) who had anything to whisper in his ear about Geoff Bendix or Robert Smart. He knew he had no chance of nailing Smart without at least one cast-iron witness. Geoff had been a recipient of Smart's loan sharking services and, if he could be found, he might be able to provide enough evidence to kick off a real investigation; one with official backing that might even run to a search warrant. Doyle was pretty sure Geoff wasn't responsible for the murder at the garage, but Geoff didn't know that, and his having been on the scene might be a useful lever to get him to testify against Smart. However, until Geoff was found, all Doyle could do was keep turning over stones until something useful crawled out.

The only thing he'd uncovered so far was evidence of a racket moving drugs from the coast into town. When he'd first come to Glastonbury, he'd assumed the place would be awash with drugs, but it wasn't. Certainly, a great deal of cannabis was grown and enjoyed, but a copper on the drugs squad told Doyle Glastonbury scored well below the regional average for hard drugs.

'Mushrooms and other homegrown hallucinogens, now', he'd said, 'world class, Doyle, world class. Makes yer proud to be British, don't it?'

All the same, Doyle thought he recognized Smart's footprint in the slime under this particular stone. And if this operation was outside the drug squad's field of vision, it might well be that it was being afforded some form of protection. As in police protection.

~~~

Granny Toogood went to church on Sunday as usual. She had acquired the habit while residing at various of Her Majesty's penal institutions as it provided a rare opportunity to mingle with the other inmates. So much could be learned, exchanged, or even stolen under the cover of hymn singing. These days, however, her attendance was primarily for the purpose of hearing about likely funerals. These she would attend, sitting at the back and dabbing her eyes with a little white handkerchief, after which she'd join the periphery of the mourners and genteelly muscle her way into the wake. There, assumed to be yet another elderly relative no one dared admit they had forgotten, she would get a free tea and note the isolated and the lonely as possible targets for a future foray into 'companionship.' These excursions never failed to reassure her that she could easily find a new victim if it ever became necessary.

~~~

Monday brought a summons for Galadriel, Mrs Spottiswood, Major Dennis, and Granny Toogood to attend the Coroners Court on Thursday 17 October at 11 in the morning. Carmel said if everyone else was going, she may as well go, too. She did a quick horoscope for the event and said that, with Mars in the ascendant and Venus being complimentary, she would advise they all wear red.

~~~

Ethan Bedlow was a vigorous man in his forties who jogged every day, followed a strict vegan diet, and was determined to live forever. He had a young wife and a new child, both relatively recent acquisitions and both regarded primarily as business expenses. Ethan kept various projects on the go from his well-appointed office in town. When it came to front of house staff, he chose young and pretty, but kept a grizzled, old-school solicitor's clerk tucked away somewhere since many of his investments were discreet to the point of secrecy.

In his office on Monday afternoon, Galadriel was made comfortable on an expensive sofa while Dai, all tweed and Celtic charm, lounged by her side. After being assured the lawsuit was nothing to worry about, she was taken through some gentle legal permutations with regard to Dai's plan for Grey Havens. Ethan, wearing designer 'casual' clothes and a silver Buddhist necklet, oozed confidence and probity while using words like 'holistic' and 'empowered' instead of 'acquisition' and 'takeover'.

He was sure the ancient well was a mystery worth pursuing. Anything that old would attract lots of attention from all sorts of official bodies and was bound to be highly profitable. Even if the water was only rumoured to cure warts, that was enough in this town. Grey Havens wasn't a listed house, but it did have value as a development site, especially as it was so close to the Tor. There were planning implications, but Glastonbury was growing and could undoubtedly support another retreat of this kind.

Then, telling Galadriel once more not to worry about the lawsuit, he ushered them both out. What he hadn't told them was that he had detected a fly in the ointment: getting a large number of tourists onto the property would not be easy. Based on the OS map he'd looked at, the boundary to the land surrounding Grey Havens consisted of two small lanes. Small lanes do not for easy access make, and at the foot of the Tor itself they'd never get permission to widen them. The well, though, was situated right on the boundary with the scrapyard next door, and the scrapyard entrance was on a junction of three roads, big enough for anything. So, the key was undoubtedly the scrapyard, but he'd need time to look into that. For the present, he was quite content to hang back while Dai spent his own money propping up Galadriel. The more of his capital Dai sank into Grey Havens, the more anxious he would be to cut a deal at some point in the future. Time was on Ethan's side, which was where he liked it.

~~~

Back at Grey Havens, Dai was seriously getting on Tamika's wick. He was all over the place, poking into the house and grounds while his sidekick, Charlie Willow Walker, dug random holes at the site of the old well. Charlie was stoned most of the time, and had no idea what he was looking for even when he wasn't. And, while Galadriel seemed happy enough to let things 'harmonise organically', Tamika could see that Dai was just taking over where Geoff Bendix had left off. She wasn't even allowed to do the books anymore; all her accounts had been taken away for 'evaluation' by Dai or one of his cronies.

'If we don't do something soon,' Tamika told Bert, 'Galadriel will be so far in that man's pocket, we'll never even get a chance to make her an offer.'

Bert agreed, so Tamika contacted the solicitor Dr Grove had recommended. As a general rule, Bert didn't take to members of the legal profession, but Mrs Danvers was quiet, competent, and treated him like a client rather than a convicted felon. She listened calmly as Tamika explained the situation and then agreed to draw up a will for Bert's approval. Then she suggested Bert cash in some insurance policies and use the proceeds to open a joint bank account with Tamika. It wasn't a huge amount but as Bert said, 'Four thousand, five hundred quid is better than a poke in the eye with a blunt stick!'

Then there was the question of where the rent on Bert's London house was disappearing to. Tamika was sure the property couldn't have stood empty all this time. Mrs Danvers told them she could find out what was going on but warned it might be a case for the police if Geoff was embezzling from his father.

'Bloody well do it' said Bert, moderating his language somewhat in front of his new brief. 'It'll just be one more thing on the list and serve the bugger right.'

Bert's will was going to be very simple. He was leaving everything to Tamika, though it was understood that Daisy would benefit as much as her mother. Mrs Danvers suggested Tamika get an accountant to ensure her tax liabilities were minimised. Before they left, she wrote out the name of her own accountant.

'He has an office in Wells and is used to dealing with all sorts of people,' she said, giving Tamika a wink, 'but he's straight as a die and a good person to have on your side.'

'A bit like you, then,' Tamika said with a smile as she helped Bert on with his jacket.

~~~

Dai was unimpressed with the results of Charlie Willow Walker's efforts. He had found a lot of stones while mostly stoned and they didn't mean a bloody thing. Galadriel suggested hiring Desmond as he already knew quite a bit about the well. When asked, Desmond was more than delighted to take over the initial excavation of the well head. However, this involved

Dai in yet more expense. His hand was always in his pocket these days and he still had his seekers to attend to. After all, it was their visits to the mystic sites and sights of Glastonbury that were funding all this. Still having received no affirmative action from Ethan Bedlow, Dai was getting anxious.

~~~

One morning, Mrs Spottiswood, Carmel, and a friend of theirs called Goldenberry (real name Irene) were doing tarot readings for Galadriel and Doris over tea and cakes in the kitchen. Suddenly Goldenberry pulled a pained expression and said, 'Ooh, smell that. Nasty, not nice.' She always maintained that she was blessed with a psychic sense of smell. 'Clairalience,' she called it, the ability to detect spiritual odours. Carmel immediately got out a crystal to try and determine if it were really some kind of manifestation.

It was, but Galadriel already knew what kind. 'Oh my God,' she cried, 'the fucking cess pit is overflowing again! Geoff said he'd fixed it!'

The soil pipes ran into a septic tank under one of the lawns downhill from the house and sure enough the overflow was leaking. It hadn't been emptied in years and Geoff's bodged stopgap had come undone. Somewhat abashed, the women tried to continue their interaction with the forces of the cosmos, but the smell quickly became intolerable. Finally, Doris said her dad knew someone who cleaned out cess pits and she was asked to call him.

Doris's dad recommended a man named Stan, who, when contacted, said he could be at the house first thing in the morning, but it would cost extra as it was an emergency.

Dai was then notified and, faced with the dreadful alternative of trying to clear the thing himself, agreed to pay Stan £100 cash.

The next day, the sun rose on a lovely, early autumn morning, all mellow fruitfulness and no mist, though there was definitely something of a miasma. Stan arrived in an ancient honey wagon and did things with large rubber hoses. One went into the huge cement cavity under the lawn, after which he calmly delved and smoked his pipe while everyone else stayed indoors with the windows closed.

Everyone except Granny, that is. She was out in the garden wearing a huge pair of leather gauntlets because she had finally made up her mind to drown Galadriel's bloody cat. She had been keeping an eye on his movements and although the vile beast slept in Galadriel's room some nights now that she had moved into the house, his daytime snooze was invariably taken in the old caravan. This was a long way from the well, though, hence the gauntlets. All she had to do was quietly tape the cat flap shut, get in through the door quickly and grab the cat, then make a determined dash through the garden, and ding dong fucking dell, pussy's in the sodding well! It was the timing that was the bugger as witnesses could be so bothersome.

Then, not a dozen yards from the caravan, she saw the metal cover had been taken off the cess pit. Oh, splendid! Fate was surely on her side! A big rubber hose had been put into the pit, but there was still plenty of room for her to drop the cat in.

Keeping close to the hedge by the back of the caravan, she cautiously secured the cat flap. Then she froze and listened. All she could hear was the pulsing of the hose as it continued sucking the vile juices out of the cess pit. In one fluid motion she entered the caravan and scooped up Bast. He writhed like a demon, with strength far beyond his size and if it hadn't been for the gauntlets her hands would have been shredded. As it was, her gabardine raincoat sustained several rips and rents. But hate gave her strength, and she gripped the bastard cat tightly as she emerged from the caravan and made the short journey to the open maw of the septic tank.

She arrived just as a hose connection split. A powerful jet of liquid poo sprayed up and then, as if aimed by Providence, straight down again onto Granny's head. She saw the movement of the movements a split second before they hit her, and the shock caused her to loosen her grip slightly. It was enough. Bast erupted from her grasp, launching himself off her chest with his back claws, and was off across the garden just in time to avoid the shit shower. Her screams brought Stan running from the back of the house and he turned the pump off as quick as he could, but the damage had been done. Granny fled to her room with only a bad smell to mark her passing.

Stan poured a bucket of water on the split, took out a bicycle puncture repair kit, and soon had the pump running again. It could have been worse, he told Tamika. 'Could have gone all over the roof, and that would have been a right bastard to clean off!'

Later when he had his tea, he mused that it had been a miracle the old rubber pipe had worked at all. He hadn't used the honey wagon in years. It was unlicensed and falling to bits, but cash was cash. He had pumped the sewage into his own slurry pit with a complete disregard for any health and safety or environmental regulations. A hundred notes were all the regulations he cared about.

~~~

That same day, Ethan Bedlow visited the now deserted scrapyard. He wanted to see for himself what was shown not only on the Ordnance Survey map, but also on the official boundary map he had borrowed from the land registry office. The boundary between this property and the land belonging to Grey Havens appeared to be a wide hedge, overgrown, with some tall trees and bushes making it even wider. It took him a while to find a way through, but once he did, the well was not far away. He could see the recent signs of excavation. The well looked deep and when he dropped a stone down it there was a plop, so it had water. But what sort? That's what he needed to find out before he went much further. So, he returned to the scrapyard and waited for Joe Chapman to arrive.

Joseph Chapman had been a dowser for close on thirty-five years. Dowsing is an ancient skill and has been used for centuries to find water under the land. No one knows how it works, it just does. Mr Chapman had been employed by the Water Board, amongst others, so it was no surprise he had been recommended to Ethan Bedlow. Another plus was that he lived outside of Glastonbury, which Ethan hoped would prevent Dai from hearing about his visit to the scrapyard. For this was to be a secret dowsing. Joe Chapman was offered no explanation, just payment in cash for a verbal report. This was no surprise to Joe. He knew underground water could be a blessing or a curse, and it was none of his business which it turned out to be.

Patiently and methodically, he walked up and down and side to side amidst the heaps of cars, tyres, and junk. The twig he held twitched close by the big boundary hedge and then dipped again as he followed a path across broken land, and then again about two hundred feet away, near the entrance to the yard. He stopped and lit his pipe.

'I reckon you got an aquifer,' he said.

'What's that?' asked Ethan, who had been following him nervously.

'Water course, underground, like the veins in yer arm. Not surprising, really, but I didn't know there was one here. Of course, you got the Chalice Well and pumping station at the foot of the Tor. And the Lion's Head, of course, but this could be a secondary, all right.'

'So, the same water as in the Chalice Well?' asked Ethan, trying not to sound excited.

'Yes, possibly,' said Mr Chapman, 'full of ferrous oxide and calcium carbonate, just like the well up the road. Silly buggers think it's sacred, magic even,' he added. 'T'ain't. Just nature's plumbing.'

With that he re-lit his pipe and carefully put his dowsing rod away.

'You won't breath a word of this to anyone, will you?' asked Ethan as he handed Joe some cash. 'That was our agreement.'

'You need have no worries on that score, Mr Bedlow.'

On the way back to town, Ethan mused on the delightful fact that field boundaries were notoriously inaccurate. Big, thick hedges were simply vegetation that grew this way or that over time, not infallible indicators of property lines. And, if one happened to have two pencils, one red and one green, and a very soft rubber, a green line could become a red one. The only other bit of kit required was a small tin of cigarette ash to age the pencil marks. It also helped if you employed a wily old solicitor's clerk who knew his way around the council archives, who to pay not to notice and just how to do it. Ethan had also found out the scrapyard was the property of Bertram Bendix, not his son Geoffrey. No court in the country could include it in bankruptcy proceedings against Geoff. No, the land belonged to his old dad, and maybe his old dad could use some money. Especially if the land in question included the well.

~~~

In the wilds of Cornwall, Geoff did a few odd jobs on the farm and was paid in small change by the cheap, miserable bastard of a farmer. He kept his head well and truly down. He used a push bike to get into the nearest town, where he would wander around dressed in charity shop clothes and masked by the beard he'd grown. Even he didn't recognise the man he saw reflected in the shop windows. What a fucking comedown, he thought. But at least I'm still in one piece.

~~~

Granny, too, was lying low following her latest disastrous attempt to kill Bast, though she raged inwardly at the unfairness of it all. Her chest still hurt from the deep grooves carved into it by the bastard's back claws, and it had taken an age to get rid of the stench. And even after she'd scrubbed and scrubbed, she still had the smell in her head. She bought a jar of Vick's VapoRub to try and mask it. The strong menthol odour soothed her with its nostalgic associations. You always remember your first time, and her first had been her little brother, who had just happened to have had a cold. His eyes had been blue, like mummy's, and she'd looked into them as the life had flowed out, all the while smelling the Vick's that had been smeared on his chest. Taking frequent huffs from the jar, she made up her mind to look forward to her next success rather than back on her recent failures. She would pay careful attention during Miss Browne's talk on poisonous houseplants next day.

*Chapter 12*

There was a good crowd at The Friends' Meeting House for Miss Browne's lecture, and the woman had brought lots of examples of toxic houseplants. However, as the talk progressed and bits of leaf and flower were carefully passed around the audience, Granny was overwhelmed by a sense of déjà vu. Then she went icy cold as the memory came back. Of course! She had seen Miss Browne before—was it Holloway or later? She racked her brain. Where was it she'd been put to work in a vegetable garden? A woman had come and explained stuff about medicinal herbs. Yes, by God, it was her! Older now, of course, but most definitely her. And if Granny could recognize Miss Browne, then Miss Browne could recognize . . . suddenly she realised a pile of plant material had built up on her lap and she hurriedly passed it on. Had anyone noticed? Get a grip, Mildred, she said to herself, and pay attention because you might need this information urgently. She tried to listen but was too distracted to take in much. Luckily, the efficient Miss Browne had typed out a list of poisonous houseplants and their associated dangers for everyone to take home with them. Granny took one when the meeting broke up and quickly left, telling Mrs Spottiswood she had some shopping to do and would catch the bus back to Grey Havens.

~~~

On Sunday, Carmel took Doris to her first spiritualist meeting. 'Will there be ghosts and that there ectoplasm stuff?' she asked excitedly as they climbed the stairs to a room above a hairdresser's shop.

'No,' said Carmel, 'Mrs Gummage won't have any of that nonsense. Her spirit guide is very correct. A Miss Harwood who was a school mistress when she was on this side. And there's to be a visiting medium today, a Mr Dunbar. Mrs Gummage tells me his spirit guide is an American Indian. A lot of them are, for some reason.'

In the large room they entered, many scented candles had been lit in an unsuccessful attempt to mask the smell of hair perming chemicals. Chairs were arranged in a circle, with a small table in the middle bearing a bowl of flowers and four silver candlesticks. It was all very tasteful and reminded Doris of visiting her gran's farm. She sat between Carmel and a very nice older gentleman. When he found out this was her first time 'in circle', he told her not to mind if she didn't get a contact right away.

Then the lights were dimmed, and Mrs Gummage rose to her feet, gave them all a warm welcome, and asked that they remain silent unless questioned by the spirits. She introduced her fellow medium, Mr Dunbar, a small, fidgety man who reminded Doris of a mouse. They were asked to hold hands. Carmel's hand was warm, plump, and slightly moist, but the man on her other side had strong, dry hands, like her dad's.

The flickering candlelight illuminated only the faces of those sitting around the table. Mrs Gummage asked those on the other side to come forth from their realms of light to illuminate those on this side of the great divide. Then she went silent, gave a bit of a shiver, and in clipped, bossy voice, started communing.

'Is there anybody out there who would like to speak with anybody in here?'

Well there was, of course, since many at the seance were regulars. George's late wife, Mabel, said she was getting on fine and advised him to see to the greenfly on his roses. Mrs Crowther chatted with her dead sister-in-law, Amelia, who said she didn't miss the world of the living one little bit. Various people drifted in and out of these kindly if dull psychic conversations, but there were no messages for Doris or the nice man sitting next to her.

Eventually, Mr Dunbar took a turn. Doris saw his head go back and his mouth drop open, then he shook himself like a dog coming in from the rain. After that he straightened up and somehow looked a lot bigger. His spirit guide being a member of the 'original people,' his voice became gruff, almost guttural.

'Is there anyone here with the name George? I get the name George coming through.'

No George.

'It could be Georgette. Does anyone here know a Georgette? She is telling me she liked pansies.'

Someone owned up to having an auntie who might have been called Georgette, though they rather thought it had been Georgina, whom they seemed to recall liking pansies, but it may have been sweet peas; it was difficult to remember because she was only a child when this auntie had passed over. The message was: 'Look out for a man with crossed eyes. He will be up to no good.'

Mr Dunbar was not having a good session. Names were floated that landed nowhere and he seemed to have lost heart. Then something changed. His voice for a start. It became more English, more 'normal,' thought Doris.

'I have a Daniel,' it said. 'He crossed over some years ago. Does anyone here know a Daniel?'

Doris felt the hand of the man on her right tighten, but he said nothing.

'I'm being shown a branch,' continued the voice. 'No, not a branch, a twig. Shape of the letter Y.''

The man next to her spoke. 'I knew a Dan. Knew him well.'

'He's laughing. Now he's saying . . . no, he's singing . . . 'water, water everywhere, nor any drop to drink.' And he says you need to finish what you started.'

There was no more.

Lights were turned on, tea was served, and the plate for donations was passed around. The man next to Doris didn't eat anything, just sat there looking thoughtful. She asked him if he was all right.

He smiled at her and said, 'I've been coming here for months. My wife used to be a member of this group and I always drove her here, but never came in. When she died, I sort of took her place, out of respect for her, I suppose.' Then he leaned over and whispered, 'To tell the truth I used to think it was all a lot of hogwash. But now I'm not so sure.'

'My friend reads palms and crystals and things. She's very psychic. A lot of the people where I work are.'

'Where do you work?'

'Oh, you probably wouldn't know it. It's just outside of town, a place called Grey Havens. It's a sort of home for the elderly but we mustn't call it that or Galadriel, she's the owner, gets all cross.'

'Grey Havens. Is that the big house up Basketmaker's Lane?'

'Yes, that's it,' replied Doris.

'My name is Joe Chapman. I wonder if I could visit sometime. There's a bit of land there I'd like to examine.'

Carmel, who had been listening, was intrigued. Putting down her cup of tea, she leaned across and said, 'I'm a resident at Grey Havens. It's not a nursing home, it's a sanctuary, but what interests you about it?'

'Long story,' said Joe, 'and now's not the time, but here's my card.' Handing it to her, he added 'I think it may be important.'

When Camel read 'Joseph Chapman, Dowser' on the card, she became even more intrigued. She gave him the phone number for Grey Havens and advised him to ask for Galadriel or Tamika. She also said she would give him a Tarot card reading for free when he visited.

On the drive home Doris asked Carmel what she thought it was all about.

'Well, my dear, I don't really know, but you must remember that what we hear in a séance is sometimes a bit obscure. Those on the other side don't or can't always make themselves clear. An adept must then ponder on the answers, seeking other avenues.'

Doris was impressed.

'And mind you don't tell anyone what you heard,' warned Carmel. 'Messages from the beyond are secret.'

Doris promised not to tell. She'd tell her mum of course. Doris told her mum everything, mostly.

Joe Chapman drove home to his empty house. After several

months, his grief was still very raw. His wife's death had been a blessed release, of course, but that was only so much comfort as he sobbed into one of her cardigans in the early hours of most mornings. There was only the faintest scent of her left in it. His daughter and son were both lovely, but one was in Australia and the other in Scotland, and his life seemed all the emptier for their absence.

The message from Dan had been totally unexpected. Though he believed he didn't believe in such things, there had been a small part of him that had hoped for some message from, some contact with, the woman he had loved for over half his life. And instead it had been Dan bloody Stone who had 'opened the veil'! Dan, who had been his partner in grime, always drunk, always moaning about something, never ready on time, but still the best damned dowser in the county. He could find water, electric cables, and where the dog pissed last Saturday. Somehow Joe knew his message was related to the job he'd recently done for that solicitor bloke, but what had he actually started? He'd found an aquifer, but that wasn't exactly unusual. He'd have liked to trace it to its source, but the man had seemed anxious to get rid of him. He'd seemed even more anxious to keep the dowsing a secret, but who from? Joe had bought some tyres for an old van from that yard a year or two before and it hadn't been Mr Smooth who'd sold them to him. He got out a huge Landplan OS map, biggest scale you could get, and spread it on his dining room table. Chinese takeaway forgotten, beer cans put aside, Joe Chapman began his own investigation of the 'other side'. Except in this case it was the other side of that ruddy great hedge.

~~~

Bert and Tamika had another meeting with their solicitor on Monday afternoon. Mrs Danvers had found out Bert's house was being rented to someone who was in turn sub-letting rooms to a whole gang of other poor sods. The rent money was going to an estate agent whom Mrs Danvers had informed of the facts regarding ownership of the house.

'I was going into town anyway,' she said, 'so I thought I would take a minor detour to see your house. I just parked outside, but it obviously has multiple occupancy. I don't know what the inside is like, but I did make some enquiries with a local estate agent and apparently it would fetch around sixty thousand as it stands. Ex-council houses always sell well, and I was told that if it came on the market, you would clear at least fifty-five thousand after various expenses.'

Bert was shocked. 'Strewth,' he said. (For some reason Bert always moderated his language around Mrs Danvers, which made Tamika smile.) 'I only paid about four grand for it. That ain't a bad turn of a shilling, now, is it?'

Mrs Danvers continued. 'Speaking as one who has been through something similar, my advice is that if you do decide to sell, then just put it on the market as it is. You get a bit less but have none of the aggravation of trying to get painters and decorators in and all that hassle. Of course, the tenants will have to be moved on, but as they're living there without the owner's permission and there is unlikely to be any tenancy agreement, that should not be a problem.'

Bert looked at Tamika. She nodded and said, 'It's your decision, Bert.'

Turning to Mrs Danvers, he said, 'Okay, I know it'll cost, but can you handle it from here? Sort it all out?'

She could. It wasn't what she usually did, but she liked this old man, and his companion, too.

As they drove back to Grey Havens, Tamika put it to Bert that he could always move back into his house if he wished. Or sell it and buy a bungalow or a place in a real retirement home.

He repeated what he had said before. 'Grey Havens suits me, Tamika. If you can get a handle on things it will be as good a billet as I could find anywhere. With a few grand up yer skirt, girl, you can do the business. Go into partnership with Galadriel. Buy her out, even.'

'There's not enough for that,' said Tamika, 'but there's enough to make a difference.'

When they got back, she found that Galadriel had gone out, no one knew where. She'd left a message with Doris asking Tamika to do the evening meal. 'Bloody cheek,' thought Tamika. Now she'd be late home and Auntie would have to collect Daisy from school. As she chopped vegetables, she wondered what was or was not happening with Galadriel and Dai's new arrangement. He appeared to be paying Desmond to fix leaking taps, blocked sinks, and innumerable other irritations in addition to digging around the well, but the bills were beginning to pile up again. When she pointed this out to Galadriel, all she said was 'I'll give them to Dai. He'll sort them.' It was the same formula as when Geoff Bendix had been around, just a different man. Of course, Tamika knew Galadriel was preoccupied with the inquest on Thursday, and there had been another snotty letter from the solicitors in Eastbourne, this time demanding all the late Mrs Meldrum's possessions be catalogued, packed, and made available for collection after the 17th.

It disturbed kind-hearted Doris to see Tamika looking so serious, so she offered to stay late and help, then attempted to cheer her up by describing the séance, but without breaking her promise to Carmel. This made her fairly incoherent, but Tamika gathered she had met a nice man with sad eyes who wanted to look around the garden because his friend on the other side had said something that made him think he ought to. Then the potatoes boiled over and they both got distracted.

Late the next morning Tamika remembered Doris's story when she took a call from Joe Chapman. He introduced himself and asked if he could look over the grounds. He didn't offer much explanation, but he was polite, and Tamika liked the sound of his voice. She thought Galadriel would have no objection (she was out again, naturally), so said yes, but not this week and just call first, please. When Galadriel eventually returned, Tamika mentioned it to her, but she only muttered something that sounded like 'Okay, if he must,' and went to her room.

Galadriel had been to Dai's. She had sat in his grubby office, which was also his dining room, and showed him the latest solicitor's letter.

'Look, Dai, I'm really worried about Thursday and I can't take any more of these horrible letters' she wailed.

'Now don't worry your head about those letters, my pet,' said Dai, his voice as smooth and melodious as a Welsh choir. 'Remember, Ethan said you have nothing to worry about, nothing at all.'

'But what if they find me guilty of something on Thursday?'

'Don't be daft, it's an inquest not a trial,' he snapped, then quickly recovered his charm. 'Besides, there's nothing you can be found guilty of, apart from caring for people, and there's no law against that. Plus, I'll be with you. Nothing nasty can happen, I promise.'

'But there's nasty things happening now! I keep getting bills, some of them overdue, and I don't even know what I've got in the bank because you have all my books.'

'It's all in hand,' he said soothingly. 'Just getting my ducks in a row. We'll have everything sorted, soon, I guarantee it.'

Galadriel said nothing, just sat disconsolately toying with some quartz pebbles that had fallen out of a small cloth bag.

'Very lucky those' said Dai. 'Lots of earth energy. Take 'em. Do you good, they will.'

'Money in the bank would do me better, Dai.'

'Soon my lovely, soon' he said, giving her his most earnest expression.

'Well, it bloody well better be,' said Galadriel and got up to leave.

Dai rose to his feet to see her out and, as he did so, picked up a small, shrink -wrapped package.

'Here take some of this,' he said placing it in her hand. 'Young Charlie reckons it the best he's smoked in years. A real cracking blend, give you a good mellow. Put on some music, relax, and let mother nature do her stuff, eh? And don't worry about Thursday. I'll be there to collect you all in the people carrier at ten.'

Galadriel drove home only slightly appeased. She could recognize bullshit, she just seemed to be powerless against it. Fucking men, she thought, as she parked up outside Grey

Havens. All talk and no do, apart from a lot of willy waving. She came to the conclusion that the only masculine thing in her life with any 'do' in it was Bast. He might not have any actual balls anymore, but he certainly did things. She retired to her room, rolled a joint, and put on some Pink Floyd. *'Hanging on in quiet desperation is the English way,'* they sang. You know it, boys, sighed Galadriel.

~~~

Mr Crabbe had decided Thursday would be a good day to visit Glastonbury and talk to the hippy woman and Bendix's father. He had also decided he needed an assistant on this trip. Not because he couldn't handle a confrontation on his own, but he did like to have a fall guy. Someone who might be remembered, whereas he would make damned sure he wouldn't be. And he always knew where to find keen young men who would do anything for the right amount of money. Posh people might have access to recruits via a network of old school or university chums, but Mr Crabbe had access to members of one of the far-right fascist groups. Lads who were considered too extreme by most of the other swastika-loving loonies. Such factions always needed money and were happy to supply storm troopers to do any amount of dirty work. Then, of course, there was the Old Lag's Employment Bureaux, which represented every prison, remand home, and secure madhouse in the country. They provided a more civilised work force with, by and large, fewer and better tattoos, though some of them did turn out to be a little erratic on the job. Well, horses for courses. He would employ someone to hire a car, be the muscle, and carry the can if need be. With Gilbert and Sullivan playing on his stereo, he lit a cigar and went over his scheme again.

~~~

Back at Grey Havens, Granny was scheming, too, as she sat in the summer house and knitted. She needed to get rid of Miss Browne before the woman recognised her. It wouldn't be easy, but there was one foible Granny thought she could take advantage of: the woman's tea. It was her own special herbal blend. No one else drank it and there was always a jar in the kitchen for Tamika or Doris to use when they made her breakfast. She thought of the list of dangerous houseplants her victim had so kindly supplied. It would be highly satisfactory to use one of the woman's own plants to kill her. Granny packed up her knitting and headed back to her room to study the list. She reached the door of the house just as an elderly lady on a bicycle arrived.

'Do you live here?,' the woman asked. 'I wonder if you could help me. I made these for Miss Browne as a wee thank-you for such an interesting talk on Saturday. I have to run and pick up my grandson from school now, though. Would you be so kind as to give them to her?'

And without waiting for an answer, she shoved a white cardboard box into Granny's hands. It had a cellophane window through which she could see four small cakes.

'They're Maids of Honour,' the woman yelled over her shoulder as she pedalled away. 'I do hope she will enjoy them!'

Granny beamed as she carried them up the stairs and into her room. Forget tea, she thought. It would be well worth using some of her precious tincture of aconite to spike the cakes and leave them outside Miss Browne's room for her to find.

And Thursday would be the perfect day to do it. Most of the residents would be attending the inquest, and Miss Browne always spent Thursday morning at her book club, returning about 11. Just the right time for a cup of tea and a cake or two!

A Glastonbury Tale

*Chapter 13*

Thursday dawned overcast and drizzly. First to set off that morning was Mr Crabbe. He met his man outside Woodford underground station early as arranged. The fellow had hired a car, so there would be nothing to link Mr Crabb with the vehicle. His 'bob a job' man for today had been baptised Vincent Pottinger some forty-eight years previously and had never set foot inside a church since. He had set foot on the rooves of plenty, however, in order to steal the lead from them. In fact, it was a fall from a church roof during one of these excursions that had caused his little problem. Opinion was divided as to whether it was stormy weather or high background electrical fields that played hell with the metal plate in Vincent Pottinger's head, but after a few years of incarceration the authorities deemed him safe enough to be let out on licence provided he continued to take his medication. The one thing he couldn't shake off was a fear of lightning, but apart from that and the fact he was a compulsive thief, he was fine. A very large man with a jolly face, he looked like the sort of vicar who always tries to see the good in people. He went berserk only occasionally, though at those times, rather than trying to see the good in people, he tried to see how quickly they could come apart. Today, under a huge mackintosh, he was dressed in a suit and tie and, thanks to the regime in Broadmoor, highly polished shoes. Mr Crabb noted this with approval, and they set off for Glastonbury.

~~~

The inquest on Mrs Meldrum was being held in the town hall, a magnificent piece of civic architecture. It was not normally used as a court, but the coroner had decided this building would be more convenient than the usual courthouse in Taunton. It was certainly grander, and Glastonbury was a better watering hole.

Dai arrived at Grey Havens in his people carrier at 10 a.m. as arranged. Getting all the residents into the vehicle was like herding cats, but eventually, after Carmel had had her last-minute desperately needed pee and Granny had made a quick trip upstairs ostensibly to get her hat (but in reality to put the cakes on the little table outside her neighbour's door), they were ready to go. Bert chose to travel in Tamika's car so he could smoke.

~~~

It was nice and quiet after everyone left. Doris mooched about pretending to hoover the hall; it would be break time soon and she'd go outside for a smoke. The front doorbell rang. She turned off the machine and opened the door.

Mr Crabbe had his clipboard and Mr Pottinger had his smile. Brandishing the clipboard, Crabbe pushed past Doris, saying he was there on official business and needed to see the owner. He was polite, but only just. Mr Pottinger simply stood there smiling, his huge bulk almost blocking the door.

Doris tried to explain the owner wasn't there, but the man

with the clipboard just kept walking. With her fluttering in his wake, Mr Crabbe went through all the downstairs rooms, including Galadriel's office. He couldn't find anything useful there, however, as all the paperwork was in such a muddle. There was no sign of Geoff Bendix and not even banging on all the doors of the first-floor rooms and shouting 'fire officer!' produced Bendix Sr. He sent his companion upstairs to check the rest of the house while he went down into the utility room and then up again to the kitchen where Doris had fled.

Mr Pottinger started on the top floor. He tried one door with no results and was trying the second one when he noticed a small box of cakes on a table. His orders had been explicit: 'No church roofs, no breaking and entering, and no violence unless specifically requested.' Nothing about cakes. He liked cakes. He picked up the box and slid it into the capacious inner pocket of his mackintosh.

~~~

As they neared the town hall, the Grey Havens contingent could see long lines of people waiting to enter. There was seating for over 200 people in the big hall, with a small stage at one end. Bright, airy, and lit by chandeliers, it was as much a theatre as a centre of local government. In fact, someone had decided that the stage would be the perfect place for the coroner and his associates to sit. At the foot of the stage, two tables had been set up for the 'learned council', and the front row of seats was reserved for witnesses. A uniformed constable at the front door was holding the crowd at bay. Dai shepherded his party up, explained that they were witnesses, and they were let in.

Ushering Galadriel and the rest to the front, Dai greeted

Ethan Bedlow who came across to assure Galadriel one last time that there really was nothing to worry about. He somehow managed to get himself introduced to Bert Bendix, giving him a gracious smile, and saying how nice it was to meet him at last. Tamika couldn't imagine why. Then he then went to sit at one of the top tables.

Already sitting at the other was Augustus Soames, BA (Cantab). His large domed scalp rose through a band of colourless hair that shed dandruff on his black three-piece suit. His heavy jowls and massive, bushy eyebrows were complemented by a huge roseate nose wedged between little piggy eyes. Sitting beside him was a much younger man whose servile attitude clearly marked him as the great man's assistant.

Other witnesses arrived and the front row began to fill up. DS Doyle came in clutching a file of papers and gave Tamika a brief nod before sitting down. A youngish, scruffy man carrying a large briefcase turned out to be the medical examiner, and a reporter from the local paper darted about collecting names and 'fuck off's. Then the general public were let in and the remaining seats were soon filled.

It was a typical Glastonbury crowd: brightly coloured clothes, flowing hair, beads, and talismans abounded, with here and there a black-robed witch or seer. As Galadriel heard the chatter and was greeted by people she knew, she thought, 'Only in Glastonbury,' and smiled despite her nervousness.

The PC who had been on the door came forward and silenced the chatter with the traditional proclamation, 'Be upstanding! This coroner's court is in session!'

Everyone rose as the coroner, flanked by two assistants, walked onto the stage. Dr Cyril Poynton was a short man, but not a small one, he had the rare gift of gravitas without pomposity. Familiar with all forms of death, whether sudden, sordid, or merely sad, he always stood firmly on the side of the deceased. He addressed his audience in a clear, well-modulated voice.

'It is not the duty of this court to apportion blame. This is a fact-finding process. Although there are lawyers sitting to represent the interested parties, there is no prosecution or defence.'

Then he laid out the facts pertaining to the demise of Mrs Irene Meldrum. The police were called, and Doyle gave his evidence, aided by Sally's photographs of the hall and stairs. Also passed around were pictures of poor Mrs Meldrum just as she had been found, with her head sticking out through the stair rails.

The medical examiner described the physical damage to the deceased and said the actual cause of death had been a broken neck. There had been a slight trace of alcohol in her blood, but so little it had probably not contributed to the fall. There were no indications of any medical condition that would have been a factor in the death.

The coroner read out the statements from Major Dennis and Granny Toogood and must have been satisfied with them because he didn't call them to give evidence in person. He did, however, call Galadriel.

He asked her if she knew whether Mrs Meldrum had had a local doctor. Galadriel was unaware of one. Had the deceased ever complained of blacking out or fainting? No, never, Galadriel was sure of that. Grey Havens was a small, caring community. They would all have known if that had that been the case. There was a murmur of agreement from the residents in the front row.

Then it was the turn of the bereaved relatives or their representatives to have their say. Augustus Soames rose to his feet and grasped the lapels of his jacket. With a booming voice and sweeping gestures as if he were addressing the bench in the Old Bailey, he described the anguish of the deceased's sister. She was devastated that the one relation she had left in the entire world had come to such an untimely end. An end brought about by the PERILOUS CONDITIONS of the stairways and floor coverings in her place of abode. A place that, far from being a home, had become a house of danger. Danger brought about by the TOTAL ABSENCE of adherence to the principals of (his voice was now a roar) HEALTH AND SAFETY!

A murmur of anger flowed through the audience and Galadriel and Major Dennis started to rise to their feet. The coroner motioned them to sit down. Turning to one of his assistants, he asked if there was any evidence that put any liability for this death down to a floor covering or any other defect in or around the stairs. There was none. Then, after another brief conference with his assistants, he addressed the court.

'All relevant witnesses having been interviewed; I am now prepared to give my verdict in this case.'

Before he could begin, however, a voice from the back of the hall called out, 'What about Mrs Meldrum? Why don't we ask her what happened?'

This suggestion was greeted with cries of 'Yes!', 'Yes, of course!', 'She can tell us if she tripped or not!' from the rest of the audience.

A tall, thin woman stood up and offered the court her services. She was dressed entirely in black, with long black hair cascading down over a profusion of black jewellery. She informed the coroner she was a registered medium and a senior member of the British Council of Mediums and as such was more than competent to contact the lady who was now on the other side.

She was interrupted by a short, round lady wearing a red knitted turban and coat that made her look like a tea cosy. She proclaimed herself the best practitioner of the Ouija board anywhere, and if the coroner would give her half an hour to nip back home, she'd bring it here and prove it to him.

An uproar ensued as practitioners and diviners of every persuasion simultaneously offered their services and rubbished all the others. The volume increased as tempers shortened.

The coroner sat stunned for a brief moment. It was like watching an affray in an aviary. Then he motioned to the uniformed constable, who eventually silenced the mob by bellowing 'Order! Order! Quiet, please!' so loudly they could no longer hear each other's competing claims.

The coroner rose and in tones that filled the now silent hall said, 'It is my belief and therefore the verdict of this inquest that the deceased, Mrs Irene Gladys Meldrum, died as a result of falling down the staircase in her place of abode. Sadly, this is all too common amongst the elderly and one can only advise caution. Therefore, I pronounce this to be an Accidental Death.'

~~~

Mr Crabb was getting nowhere with Doris. All his questions just seemed to confuse her. As far as he could gather, the entire household had either been arrested or carted off by some Welsh bloke. He was contemplating killing her when Mr Pottinger came back into the kitchen. He had searched everywhere and was certain there was no one else in the place. They left.

On the journey back to Woodford, Mr Crabbe contemplated his next move. His client would not be happy, but few investigations were ever straightforward. The motorway was fairly busy, but Mr Pottinger handled the car well. They had negotiated the M5 to the M4 and were making good time. The road ahead was clear, so Mr Pottinger withdrew the slim white box from his coat pocket and offered it to his employer. Thinking it was something the man must have brought along with him as a means of ingratiating himself, Crabbe murmured thanks and opened the box. Cakes! Small delicate cakes that looked all very nice, but to a diabetic were poison. He grunted a no thank you and thrust the box back in the direction of his driver, who eyes on the road, taking one in his big beefy hand, crammed it into his mouth.

The crash was on the six-o'clock news. One lane of the Eastbound M4 just before Swindon was blocked. A saloon car had ploughed into the back of a petrol tanker. The tanker driver had been airlifted to hospital, but all that remained of Mr Crabbe and Mr Pottinger were two crispy corpses whose startlingly white teeth grinned against the charred remains of their faces. The police could find no reason for the accident. They said they just wished drivers would heed the road signs that advised them 'Tiredness can kill, take a break.'

*Chapter 14*

For the inhabitants of Grey Havens, the ride home was almost jolly despite the occasion. The verdict had brought a sense of relief and they all felt it was time to move on, though nobody actually said so. Tucked in the back seat, Granny was focussed on finding out whether her anonymous gift had done the job on her latest victim. She was the last one out of the van and she hung about while the others went straight up to the comfort of their own bathrooms. When the stairs were clear, she almost ran up the three flights to the top floor where she could see...yes, the box had been taken! But had the contents been eaten? It was a waiting game now and she kept to her room, ears strained for any sound that might herald the last agonized moments of Miss Browne. It was a vigil she was only too happy keep.

Mrs Spottiswood and Major Dennis came down for a bit of supper later and were joined by Carmel. Bert was having an early night after eating a microwaved pasty. Doing the washing up afterwards, Tamika asked Doris if things had been quiet when they were all out. Doris said a man had called, she thought he might have been from the council, but he wasn't nice, and he had a friend with him who smiled at her in a funny way. When Tamika asked if she'd let them in, Doris said no because she didn't want to get into trouble.

The following morning a large Mercedes-Benz purred up to the front of Grey Havens and decanted the portly shape of Mr Augustus Soames. His small, shiny black shoes sank into a puddle and he looked down in distaste. Then he looked up in distaste and sideways in distaste. It was the only look he had. All of Mrs Meldrum's possessions were ready and waiting for him in the big lounge. Tamika had typed the list Major Dennis made when they packed them. If Mr Soames had been going to question it, the look on Tamika's face made him change his mind. With the loading of those last few goods and chattels, the life and times of Mrs Meldrum finally came to an end.

With this melancholy thought, Tamika went back to the office. Lacking the official account books, she had been trying to work out the various cash flows from memory. She was sure Grey Havens was viable. Not a huge earner, no, but viable. All that was lacking was enough capital and ambition to do the necessary work.

Suddenly Tamika realized she was shivering. She checked the radiator. It was cold. That bloody boiler again, she thought. Yet another of Geoff's scrapyard specials.

~~~

Granny had endured a long, sleepless night. She hadn't heard any sounds coming from Miss Browne's room, which was a good sign but inconclusive. However, she could think of no logical excuse for checking on the woman and besides, she certainly didn't want to be the one to find her dead. She was impatiently waiting for someone to come see why Miss Browne hadn't turned up for breakfast when there came a soft tap on her door. This was a surprise; no one ever visited her room. She was even more surprised when she answered it and saw Miss Browne standing on the threshold. All the lovely visions of her lying on her bedroom floor curled up like knotted string as the result of an excruciating death vanished in an instant.

Something of her disappointment must have shown on her face because Miss Browne hurriedly said 'Oh, I do hope I'm not disturbing you. I just wondered if you had noticed the lack of heating and hot water this morning.'

Granny, dismayed by yet another failure, simply stood, stony-faced, in the doorway. Miss Browne thought perhaps the woman hadn't heard her. She raised her voice and spoke as clearly as she could. 'Do you have any heating? Mine seems to be off.'

Then, looking past Granny into the room, she noted its spartan condition. The small, iron-framed bed had been made with unusual precision, as if ready to be inspected. The sink and work surface of the small kitchen area were empty and spotless. There were no photographs or pictures on the walls, no ornaments anywhere. And someone had defaced a rather nice, probably Edwardian wardrobe with a hasp and padlock.

Granny still hadn't moved or said anything. One part of her wanted to reach for the very sharp knives she kept in the wardrobe and another part just wanted this woman out of her space.

Miss Browne shivered, then summoned all her good nature to say, 'My dear, what a delightful little home you have here. You must let me give you some plants for your windowsill. Such good friends they become, you know, and they never talk back,' she added with a nervous chuckle, then fled with no further mention of the heating.

~~~

All of the downstairs radiators were cold. Tamika went to the utility room and checked the huge old boiler. Nothing. No sign of flame, which made sense when she looked at the fuel dial. No bloody oil. She had told Galadriel they were running low and she'd said she'd get Dai to order some. It was October now, the nights got chill, and the house was full of elderly people who needed warmth. She took a small fan heater to Bert's room, then went down to the kitchen to find Carmel holding Galadriel's hand. She was reading her palm.

Despite her irritation, Tamika paused in the doorway for a moment. She had to admit it: Carmel was good. She peered into Galadriel's hand, then looked up into her eyes and down again, tracing the lines with a serious expression, full-on gypsy mystic. When Tamika finally spoke, both Carmel and Galadriel jumped.

'I hope you can see the bit in the future where they deliver the heating oil that useless bastard Dai Griffiths was supposed to order. It's cold, the tank's empty, and we haven't got enough electric fires to go around.'

'I thought it was chilly this morning,' said Carmel brightly. 'And there was no hot water.'

Galadriel got quickly to her feet. 'He's probably forgotten. I'll phone him now, don't make a fuss.' She hurried off, leaving Tamika and Carmel looking at each other.

'Funny, that,' said Carmel. 'I was just about to tell her I saw conflict ahead, but also opportunity on the horizon. Then you came in.'

Tamika found Galadriel in her office, phone in hand, staring at nothing. 'I can't get hold of Dai,' she said. 'Apparently he's in Wales visiting relatives. He's not expected back until next week.'

'Now's the time,' thought Tamika. Her and Bert's resources were not really enough, not yet, but never mind. They could make a start. Put themselves in the frame, at least.

'I'll phone the oil company,' she said, and proceeded to use her own credit card to pay for half a tank, which brought her almost up to her credit limit. Galadriel just sat there while this was going on. She had a gift for looking facts in the face and still seeing fantasies.

'Thanks,' she said when Tamika had hung up. 'I'll get Dai to pay you back as soon as he returns.'

'Oh yes? And will he? Or will he just string me along as he has you? And what if I need to get Daisy shoes in the meantime? How am I supposed to pay my own bills?'

Galadriel wasn't interested in reality. 'I'm sure when Dai comes back next week, he'll sort it all out.'

But Tamika wasn't letting go. Not this time.

'Listen. I've worked for you for more than four years. I like you, you're a good human being, and I know you really do want the best for everyone. But the fact is you let people take advantage of you. I know all about Geoff Bendix and his part in Grey Havens. And I know you didn't feel like you had a choice at the time, and you didn't know he was a crook. Now, with Geoff gone, you're in dire straits again and along comes Dai Griffiths, another chancer without a penny to his name.'

Galadriel started to protest, but Tamika waved her down.

'No, it's true. Dai is conning you. He wants control of this house so he can benefit *his* business, not yours. And he's planning to get rid of over half our residents, Galadriel! People you smile and say hello to every day, people you share your meals with nice people; daft maybe, a bit silly, but good people who trust you.'

Galadriel's expression didn't change, but as she sat toying anxiously with one of her necklaces, the string broke. Beads cascaded onto the top of her desk, then fell to the floor with a clatter and rolled in all directions. Perhaps it was the association with Mrs Meldrum's death or maybe she just suddenly realized what a hole she was in, but as the beads dropped, so did the tears. Slowly at first, then followed by more and more.

'I'm so fed up with these men and their promises!' she wailed. 'With Geoff disappearing like that, I didn't have anyone to turn to. Dai said he would handle everything. And I was so grateful when he sorted out the telephone bill.'

Tamika put her head in her hands so Galadriel wouldn't see her rolling her eyes.

'Oh, it's all such a mess, Tamika. And the truth is I just haven't got enough money or energy to go on struggling for much longer.'

Tamika looked up and said 'I think I have a solution. A real, long-term solution. But you'll have to trust me. Will you?'

Galadriel was so surprised she stopped crying. How could Tamika have a real, long-term solution for this situation? She was clever, yes, and a better friend than Galadriel probably deserved, but she was a single mother who lived with her auntie. How the hell could she help?

'Galadriel, please,' urged Tamika. 'Come with me.'

Bemused, Galadriel allowed herself to be shepherded up to Bert's room. Sitting in front of the TV in his pyjamas and a tattered dressing gown, he was as surprised to see Galadriel in his room as she was to be there, but he cottoned on immediately.

Groaning his way up from the sofa, he said, 'Nice to see you ladies. Want a drink?'

Tamika sat Galadriel down at the small table in the window. Looking out, she caught a glimpse of the Tor in a landscape of gold and green. Somehow it gave her hope.

'To what do I owe the pleasure?' asked Bert, placing a bottle of Scotch and three glasses on the table next to a full ashtray.

Tamika did most of the talking while Galadriel drank Scotch and tried to follow what was being said. After a while, Bert went to a drawer in his sideboard, brought out a cheque book, and wrote Galadriel a cheque for £2500.

'This should get you out of the shit for now,' he said. 'Both of you get down to the bank, pay this in, get a complete set of statements, and then Tamika will sort out who gets what. And you, my dear,' he said, patting Galadriel's knee, 'will advise her. Then, when that's done, we can have another chat about the future.'

Galadriel was calm now but still confused. Three stiff whiskies had achieved the former, but only added to the latter. Bert, seeing this, took her hand.

'Now just for the record,' he said, 'I'm not like that arse of a son of mine. What I say I'll do, I'll do. The money I have given you is part of Tamika's inheritance. She'll explain all that to you if she wants to.' He dropped Galadriel's hand. 'Now bugger off the pair of you and get things sorted. I'm missing Knock Out and the bint on that show reminds me of a barmaid I once knew.'

They left promptly to avoid a detailed description of exactly which parts of the lady on *Knock Out* reminded him of the barmaid. Besides, they needed to get to the bank before it closed.

The following day was a Saturday, but Tamika came in to go over the bank statements with Galadriel. She brought Daisy, who went straight up to 'Grandad's' room to do some drawing. Going over all the bills, invoices, and final demands could have been a depressing task, but somehow it wasn't. They both felt they were moving forward rather than looking back. Tamika had explained about Bert's house and the will and everything. Galadriel was still trying to get her head around the idea of Tamika doing the steering, but there was no denying it was a huge relief. While Tamika worked the calculator, Galadriel stared out of the office window and daydreamed. It was a division of labour she could certainly get used to.

*Chapter 15*

'Well, at least it's dry,' thought Doyle, who was tucked away on a rooftop overlooking a car park in a shopping centre in Bridgwater. It was technically outside his remit and by rights he should have liaised with the local police, but he was now convinced some blue-clad bastard was feeding information to Robert Smart. He looked through his binoculars. It was a Sunday morning and the car park wasn't crowded yet. The car he had followed had parked up at the end of a row of vehicles near the entrance to a supermarket. No one had got out and he could see cigarette smoke drifting from the open window on the driver's side. The driver was a scruffy, tousle-haired individual known as 'Laughing Boy' because of a huge scar around his neck. He was on record as being a dealer, possibly involved with Mr Smart. Doyle scanned the rest of the carpark. A few people came and went, mums with pushchairs going to and fro between shops and cars. Nothing out of the ordinary. Then a large Chelsea Tractor drove in. Mud splattered, with a tow hitch and a horsy sticker in the rear window, it parked up three vehicles behind Laughing Boy. The driver did not get out. Doyle waited, still scanning the whole scene, but never losing focus on those two cars. Finally, a grey Volvo Estate drove in and parked in line with the others, but at the end of a different row. Again, no one got out, but from the Chelsea Tractor there emerged a well-dressed woman in a headscarf carrying a shopping bag. She walked calmly and purposefully into the supermarket.

Doyle hadn't brought a camera with him and cursed himself for it. Other people came and went, but there was no movement from the Volvo. It wasn't long before the woman in the headscarf came out again, still carrying her original shopping bag but now with one from the supermarket as well. As she passed by Laughing Boy's vehicle she paused. The door of the car opened, and a very quick exchange of plastic bags took place. A classic 'brush contact'. If he had been distracted for even a fraction of a second, he'd have missed it. The woman then got into her vehicle, put on her seatbelt, and drove out.

As soon as she left, Laughing Boy emerged from his smoke-filled car. He sauntered over to the Volvo and passed the shopping bag through the window to the driver.

Doyle rushed down the fire escape, emerging dusty and dishevelled outside the fire door. The Volvo was almost out of the car park already, but from where he was standing, he could easily identify the driver. It was Smart all right. Getting into his own car, he moved out into the traffic, keeping the Volvo a few cars ahead. In the good old days Doyle would have had a team, three cars at least, but now he was on his own. All he could do was hope Smart didn't adopt any fancy anti-surveillance tricks. Fortunately, Smart didn't pick him up and Doyle was able to follow him to a farm some ten miles out in the Somerset Levels. Bandit country, he sighed, as he drove by the entrance. Without official sanction there was precious little he could do about Smart, but he decided then that he would risk a journey into his past and find out a little bit more of the man calling himself Robert Smart.

~~~

On Monday Bert Bendix got a love letter. It was from Ethan Bedlow, who said he really, really wanted to meet with Mr Bendix and discuss 'things to their mutual advantage'. Bert showed Tamika the letter.

'I bet it's that bloody scrapyard,' he said. 'I reckon that sneaky sod knows I own it and he wants to get his hands on it. He doesn't hang about does he. Bit too smooth for my liking,' he added, slurping his tea from a saucer. 'Still, do no harm to let him make his pitch. Find out what he's prepared to pay.'

Bert's ex-council house was now on the market and Mrs Danvers had told him there was already a buyer and it would probably be sold quite soon. Thus, selling the scrapyard was not imperative, but in view of Galadriel's financial situation, the money might be useful. Tamika spoke to Mrs Danvers about the rescue package and was told a formal partnership or even a limited company was vital. She suggested they meet, sooner rather than later, to draft an agreement.

'If you leave things hanging,' she said, 'you have no way of protecting your investment should your friend Galadriel fall under a bus.'

Of course, what she really meant was should Galadriel change her mind. Mrs Danvers said she would drive out that afternoon. There was still no sign of Dai, which was fine with Tamika. The last thing she wanted right now was him confusing Galadriel with more of his worthless promises.

~~~

Granny wandered the grounds as if doing a bit of gardening but was in fact racking her brains for a way to kill Miss Browne. Quickly. She was convinced the woman had recognized her and would soon tell the others, if she hadn't already. Granny's innate paranoia, aggravated by all her recent failures, was beginning to get the better of her. Bast slunk by and she hurled her trowel at him. She missed, of course, but it was the thought that counted.

~~~

Mrs Danvers was a pleasant surprise to Galadriel, for whom the word 'solicitor' did not conjure up an image of a middle-aged lady with short grey hair and a lot of stylish Scandinavian silver jewellery. She didn't bustle, fuss, or dither, either. She had a clear idea of what the options were and explained them to Tamika and Galadriel in a perfectly straightforward manner using no jargon whatsoever. Bert sat in the corner and didn't say much but listened very hard.

There were really only two choices: limited company or partnership. In the end there was no doubt that the best and fairest choice was to form a company. Bert, Tamika, and Galadriel would have equal shares as Bert was supplying all of the money, Tamika all of her time, and Galadriel the use of her home. It didn't escape Mrs Danvers' notice that Bert's shares would go to Tamika when he died, but Galadriel would still own the house itself, after all.

It was nearly six that evening when Mrs Danvers finally left, saying she would get things moving and they could expect to receive a letter from her soon outlining their meeting and everything that had been agreed. The three prospective directors of the new company then had a quiet cup of tea before one of them went up to his room absolutely knackered, as he put it, and the other two got on with cooking supper. Nothing seemed to have changed, but they all knew it had.

Bert was very tired the next day and thought he might be getting a cold, so he asked Tamika to talk to the Bedlow bloke and find out what he wanted. She phoned the man, but he was unwilling to discuss anything with her, it had to be Mr Bert Bendix himself. Tamika told him Bert wasn't feeling well at the moment but would give him a call when he was fit again.

Tamika went into town to see if the chemist could recommend something that might help Bert. The town being Glastonbury, her errand was complicated by a dragon. It was slowing the traffic and gathering a crowd. The entire High Street was taken up by the long, cloth-covered beast, which was being paraded by countless colourfully dressed people who were prancing all around it. Some had drums, some flutes, and others cymbals. Traffic was hooting, pedestrians were milling, and a lone policeman was policing. Tamika recognised him as the constable who had attended Mrs Meldrom's demise. Apparently, having given up on the traffic, he was remonstrating with a scruffy man in a tattered purple robe who was sitting on the sidewalk with his back to a shop window, loudly and enthusiastically banging a drum.

Tamika elbowed her way to a café and looked for a seat at an outside table. The only empty one was opposite a large, dark-haired man calmly reading a newspaper as though completely oblivious to what was going on. It was Doyle. She walked over and he looked up, smiled, and folded his newspaper. Then, after inviting her to sit down, he nodded towards Pugh.

'What you see there is an unstoppable force meeting an immovable object. The unstoppable force is young constable Pugh of the Somerset Constabulary. The immovable object is one Harry Brill or, as he is sometimes known, the Mahatma Drogon-gosh. Harry has discovered he can earn more money by banging that drum until someone pays him to move on than he ever did as a hospital porter. Until his palm is crossed with silver, he will squat, bang, and mutter. Normally the shopkeepers wouldn't mind, but he is so bloody bad at it they can only stand it for so long. Pugh can try and arrest him for obstruction, but that will only stir up the tourists, who will give him grief for persecuting a holy man. Pugh cannot win, but neither can he let it go. Meanwhile, Jimmy the Fingers and his team work the crowd.' Doyle smiled again. 'Well, they were going to, until they saw me'.

Tamika smiled and wondered why she always felt so relaxed in this man's company. He was, after all, a policeman, and she'd never felt comfortable around one of them before.

A waitress came over and coffee was ordered. Doyle asked Tamika what had brought her to town and she told him about Bert.

'That's too bad. I like the old villain. Shame my granny isn't still with us. She'd have made up a concoction that would have got him back on his feet in no time'.

'Was she a doctor?'

'Witch doctor, maybe', laughed Doyle. 'A little cottage loaf of a woman with grey hair and a jolly smile. Well, most of the time. Try and con her, though, and she'd box yer ears like she was Jack Dempsey'.

'Was this in Ireland?' asked Tamika.

'Drumskinny. County Fermanagh. Beautiful place got a stone circle all of its own'.

'Is that where you were brought up?'

'Not far from there'.

After a pause, Tamika asked, 'Why did you become a policeman? It couldn't have been an easy choice with things as they were.'

Doyle sighed. 'Long story short, I had an Uncle Bob who was a copper. I wanted to be like him, I suppose. Make some sort of difference. Didn't turn out like that, though.'

Tamika sensed this was not a road he wanted to go down and changed the subject. 'How do you like Glastonbury? It must be very different from Ireland'.

'That it is', said Doyle. 'For a start you don't get shot at. Well, not so far, anyway', he added with a rueful smile. 'When I first arrived the place seemed as mad as a box of frogs, but the people are actually very kind. And it's educational, too. I didn't know one of my chakras from another until I moved here'.

Tamika laughed, finished her coffee, and said she'd better get to the chemists before it closed for lunch. Doyle said he was ready to go, too, so they left some money on the table and walked the few yards to the shop together. A sign on the door said it was closed and would open in half an hour.

'Damn', said Tamika.

'Have you eaten?' asked Doyle.

She hadn't, and neither of them fancied a pub, so they bought cakes and took them to the Abbey where they wandered among the ruins until they found a bench in quiet spot.

'So, how's your daughter? asked Doyle. "Daisy, right?'

It may have been the influence of the ancient stones under

which monks had murmured their prayers for hundreds of years, or perhaps it was just that the secluded corner they were in made her feel safe, but Tamika found herself telling Doyle all about her family and her life. Her mother's death when she was only a few weeks old, her complete lack of a father, and her feelings about not providing Daisy with one. He did very little prompting; just enough to show he was truly listening. Then, apparently under the same spell, he told her about his own life.

'My part of Ireland is a mass of contradictions and always has been. Have you ever heard of the Belfast Blitz? During the war, the Luftwaffe bombed the shit out of Belfast. This was at a time when Northern Ireland and the Republic were deadly enemies. But the morning after the first big bombing, the Republic sent fire crews to Belfast. Seventy-one men, all volunteers. They stayed and helped for three days. That was in 1941. I grew up in a rural community that hadn't seen much of the troubles, but mixed marriages like my parents were still rare'.

'I know all about being mixed', said Tamika. 'I never really fitted in when I was young, either. Not black, not white; "the coffee-coloured kid", I was called at school.'

Doyle nodded. 'They called me a Taig at one school, so my mother got me into another one where they called me a Prod. And you couldn't tell by our accents or clothes what side of the street we came from. We were all just as scruffy and badly behaved. I joined the police force in the 60's and it was messy, but it was hard to blame either side, really. Not the ordinary people who were just trying to get on with their lives, anyway. It was the madmen and maniacs on both sides that brewed it up and kept it boiling. Of course, the stupidity of the English government didn't help'.

He looked up at the ruined arch towering above them. 'I thought then, as I do now, I'm a copper. A policeman first and foremost. Ideology, religion, the colour of someone's skin; none of that matters to me, except as it might apply to motive. The law may be an ass, but it's all we've got to protect the innocent from the evil bastards who prey on them. And I thought it would be simple, you know? I'd just nick any bastard who broke the rules. To hell with what side they were on. Even if they were army or RUC, I'd have 'em.'

He looked at Tamika. 'And that was my problem. Made me dangerous to everyone, so they put the mark on me. Bullets in the post and obituary notices written on police notepaper stuck in my in-tray'.

'But why', asked Tamika, 'if you were doing your job fairly?'

'Ah, well, you see, by that time the Troubles were no longer just political. Drugs, protection, loan sharking—big money was being made. "Free" Ireland! Not on your life. Everybody paid one way or the other. Taig or Prod, it didn't matter.'

'Is that why you left?'

Doyle ran his hands through his hair and blew out a long breath before he answered. 'My wife's brother had been mixing it with the wrong crowd. Eventually they found out about me and threatened to harm him unless I agreed to steer police attention away from their activities. I refused, but offered to protect him if he'd turn them in. He tried to do a runner instead, so of course they killed him. Because of me, my wife said. Because I wouldn't go with the flow like everyone else. A little later I was set up, probably by someone I worked with.

I got lucky, just a wound, and I nailed the man they sent. But goodbye to the province and hello sleepy Somerset. My wife stayed behind and divorced me for mental cruelty.'

After a shocked silence Tamika said, 'I'm sorry. I didn't mean to rake up such unpleasant memories.'

'No, it's all right,' said Doyle, suddenly embarrassed. 'My fault. You didn't need to hear about all that.'

They left the abbey and walked back to the chemists, then said goodbye quickly and almost formally, both uncomfortable with having shared so much with someone who was, after all, a relative stranger.

~~~

The next day, lunch at Grey Havens was dished out by Doris. There was potato and leek soup, lumps of coarse, nourishing bread, and local cheese, and there were the usual takers: Major Dennis, Carmel, and Mrs Spottiswood. Galadriel was off visiting a new bakery and cooperative where they offered wholesome food without the grit and more varieties of lentils than anywhere else in the county (she was very careful to purchase only those with a low flatulence index).

Tamika was with Bert, and Doris had left the diners to themselves when Dai walked in through the back door. Sitting himself down without even taking off his greasy leather hat, he got stuck into the provender with no more than a nod to the others.

He was famished, he told them between slurps of soup. 'Been hunting,' he said. 'Nature's bounty from the dark forests and sacred woodlands.'

More soup was slopped into his bowl and the pile of bread

on the table was reduced even further. The Major said nothing and retreated from the table. There were some things even a hardened old soldier preferred not to witness, and one of them was this oaf pillaging all the grub like a one-man Celtic invasion. Mrs Spottiswood and Carmel knew Dai and found him mildly interesting. He was a Druid, of course, and therefore part of the rich tapestry of the town.

Leaning back in his chair at last, Dai said with a contented burp, 'Best crop ever. You'd not believe it after this dry summer and all. Oh, the Goddess is good this year, she is. Never such bounty from her bosoms before, I can tell you.'

Carmel poured him a mug of tea. 'Mushrooms, is it?'

'Ah, but special mushrooms, very special indeed. Called Liberty Caps by some and Queen Mab's Nipples by others. They are magic, see?'

'You mean the ones that do your head in?' asked Mrs Spottiswood.

'Dear lady, such fungi have been used by druids and soothsayers since the hills were young. They open your mind to the cosmos and show you the hem of mother nature's gown, they do.'

Dai had been selling magic mushrooms for years—or, as he put it, offering the fruits of his mystic knowledge to other seekers of the infinite. It was a strictly cash business, no mucking about, and its proceeds were coming in extremely useful at the moment. Ethan Bedlow was not answering his calls, and it was only because of the mushrooms and some advance bookings for Samhain that he had any money at all.

Tamika came into the kitchen, saw Dai, and said, 'Galadriel isn't here.' Then, seeing there was nothing left on the table but a few crumbs and a small piece of cheese, she added, 'Or did you just stop in for lunch?'

'Actually,' said Dai, 'I've come to drop something off for Galadriel. I heard she's been trying to get hold of me and I've been away visiting a sick relative'. He winked at Carmel.

Tamika suggested they go into the office. She led, he followed. She sat down at the big desk, he sat down on the visitor's chair opposite. Taking off his hat and putting on a smile, Dai placed an envelope on the desk in front of her.

'Just topping up the pot. You probably don't need it, but it's my duty of care.' he said smugly and wound his smile up another notch.

'We don't, no thanks to you, and please be so good as to return all our account books and anything else you've taken away.' She pushed the envelope back toward Dai and added another to it. 'And here is a cheque for all the money you've loaned Galadriel to date.'

Tamika saw the look on his face change, and it was a picture. Dai was stunned.

'You're not going to get your hands on Grey Havens, Dai. Go back to fleecing your so-called seekers and hope the poor sods never find you out.'

He exploded. 'It's that slimy fucker Ethan Bedlow, isn't it? No wonder the bastard's been avoiding me! He waited until I spent all my cash and now he's slid in sideways and cut me out. Well, he'll turn you silly cows over, too, you mark my words!'

He grabbed up both envelopes and stormed out.

Tamika was certainly interested to learn that Ethan Bedlow had been working with Dai to get hold of Grey Havens. Poor Galadriel wouldn't have stood a chance with those two cunning swine trying to stitch her up. If she had felt a tiny bit sorry for Dai before, she bloody well didn't now.

~~~

In the chill, dank recesses of Cornwall, Geoff was doing what he could to keep boredom at bay. He had found a cash job in a caravan park just down the lane. He'd been riding his bike and literally ran into an old boy in a beat-up truck. The man had taken Geoff back to his bungalow where they had straightened out the bike wheel and shared a whisky. Alf came from London, was now retired, and had a few caravans in a field. No further questions asked, no further answers given, but Geoff could do a bit of maintenance at £5 an hour, cash, if he liked. There were no residents on the site now. They had all decamped before winter set in.

'Like fucking house martins, they are' said Alf. 'Make a nest, shit everywhere, then bugger off to sunnier climes.'

Geoff got on with Alf all right and the work wasn't hard, but he knew he couldn't live this kind of life forever. He considered trying to contact his father, but that was undoubtedly what both Smart and the cops were looking out for. Besides, he wasn't sure the old bastard would help him in any case.

The old bastard in question had sold his ex-council house and got a reasonable price for it, all things considered. The new company was up and running and everyone at Grey Havens seemed happy enough with the arrangement.

Even Dai had finally calmed down. Maurice's take on the whole affair was that it was a lucky escape. 'Bottomless money pit, mate,' he said, 'and you wouldn't have been your own boss.' And, after all, with the money he had given Galadriel refunded and Samhain just around the corner, there was a lot to be getting on with.

For those who follow the pagan way, the night of 31st October is the beginning of winter, or the 'darker half' of the year: Samhain, when the ghosts of the dead return to earth. It is thought that the presence of otherworldly spirits makes it easier for those who are so inclined to make predictions about the future. Feasting, bonfires, and much quaffing are involved, and Dai's celebrations were always well attended. He built a huge bonfire in a mate's field outside of town and set up a marquee. There was a hog roast, barrels of cider and beer, and flagons of local mead. Strictly 'ticket only', he and his fellow Druids put on a grand show. Over the years its reputation had grown and this year he had hired a bigger marquee and built a bonfire he reckoned could be seen from space. He had sold three hundred tickets at a fiver each and there was a waiting list. Over-eighteens only. Charlie Willow Walker had suggested a condom machine but that was vetoed by the bloke who owned the field. He reckoned it was bad enough clearing up as it was without a lot of used Jonnies littering his meadow.

All in all, Dai thought he would clear fifteen hundred on the tickets, plus sales of booze and roast hog. A nice one all round. He never personally sold drugs at these events; that was Charlie's little earner, and to maintain culpable deniability he made sure he was never involved in the transactions. Those had to take place outside the sacred site. It was while going over these rules for the umpteenth time that Dai learned of Charlie's latest mind-bending experiment: Mad Honey Mead. Charlie had a mate who had a mate who had been visiting Turkey recently and came across a special honey made by bees who frequented a certain type of rhododendron whose nectar contained a powerful, mind-bending drug.

'Told me he had some on a bit of toast on a Friday and was out of his skull till the following Wednesday,' said Charlie. 'Fucking marvellous. Saw the beginning of time and danced to the music of the spheres with Marylin Monroe and all. He gave me a tiny jar of it, and I used it to make some mead.'

Charlie Willow Walker's dad kept bees and made a good money selling his honey. Charlie got all the dregs with bits of wings and legs in and used it to make mead. He had tried adding LSD in the form of thin squares of gelatine called 'windowpanes' that dissolved in the liquid. This resulted in a drink that was full of hidden promise and certainly broadened one's horizons. Between such experiments and his constant pot smoking, it was a wonder Charlie Willow Walker could function at all. But he did, to a fashion, and was a useful member of Dai's team if only because he was cheap and did all the rubbish jobs.

~~~

The extent of Ethan Bedlow's duplicity was revealed to Tamika one afternoon when Joe Chapman finally managed to find time to visit Grey Havens. He explained what he had found on the land around the scrapyard, then Tamika and Galadriel went into the grounds with him. It became a bit of an expedition, with both of them trying their hands at dowsing under Joe's tutelage. Neither of them had the gift, which was a great source of regret to Galadriel, who always fancied herself at one with mother nature.

They showed him the well, which Joe said was the fulcrum

for the main aquifer. He then braved brambles and nettles to follow it to the edge of Galadriel's land, right where he had picked up the trace on the other side of the big hedge.

They returned to the house and Tamika brought Bert down. Joe told him all about the cunning routes by which water found its way under the land from here to the Tor. Then walking somewhat unsteadily between Tamika and Joe, he tried his hand at dowsing. He declined to go as far as the garden and stuck to the lawn closest to the house.

'I did a bit of mine clearing in the army,' he said, 'but never with a fucking stick.' Suddenly, the twig dipped. 'Weren't me!' said Bert, somewhat alarmed. 'Didn't do nothing, honest.'

Even Joe was impressed. 'It's probably a water pipe,' he said. 'That's bloody good for a beginner, though. Fancy a job?'

Afterwards, sitting in the dining room with a cup of tea, Joe brought out his huge map, which nearly covered the entire table, and went over everything they'd seen. Tamika really liked him, and when she found out he was a widower going home to a takeaway, that was it. Normally she left around now and Galadriel served the evening meal, but not today. When Joe finally got up to leave, he was full of good food and a couple glasses of wine. Tamika asked if he would come again, in his professional capacity, and advise them about the well. He gave Tamika a knowing look and said he would be delighted. 'I'll trade knowledge for a meal like tonight's anytime.'

*Chapter 16*

When he found out the scrapyard actually belonged to Bert, Desmond asked if he could continue to use the workshop so he could still earn a bit here and there fixing washing machines and such. Bert liked the lad and Tamika trusted him, so he was allowed to keep the keys to the yard and the garage. There was no electricity now, but being a clever young man, he had rigged up a generator. He was there on Saturday, tinkering away on various things, when he had a visitor.

Ethan Bedlow, dressed in a wax jacket and green wellies, with map and camera in hand, wandered into the yard and started to pace out distances and survey all that he hoped would one day be his.

Desmond's polite 'Can I help you?' was met with an indignant 'What are you doing here?' — as if Bedlow already owned the place.

A brief conversation ensued, which resulted in Ethan leaving and heading straight for Grey Havens. Tamika and Doris both had Saturdays off so the only staff on site was Galadriel. Mrs Spottiswood saw him first, however, and let him in. She remembered him from the inquest and offered him tea, but he only wanted to see Mr Bendix. Muttering phrases such as 'rough diamond', 'a bit deaf', and 'his bark is worse than his bite', she led him up the stairs, showed him Bert's door, and scarpered.

When Bert eventually heard the knocking, he turned off his television and shouted for whoever it was to 'Come in, for Christ's sake!'

Ethan entered and introduced himself, then sat down without waiting to be invited. Bert knew who he was, all right. Tamika had told him how the cunning sod had stitched up 'that shifty Welsh git', as Bert was wont to describe Dai, which was fine with Bert. But she had also told him why he was looking to buy the scrapyard, which wasn't.

Bert sat back in his big easy chair and lit a cigarette. He observed Bedlow through the smoke and was pleased to see he obviously didn't approve.

'I understand you own a small area of waste ground adjacent to Grey Havens,' Ethan began, and gave a small cough to draw Bert's attention to his sensitive lungs. 'It is mostly likely polluted with oil and heavy metals and will cause you problems with the local council. They will undoubtedly serve you a notice to clean it up before any more pollution spreads to the immediate environment.'

'What's that to you?' asked Bert.

'I know that the state of the land is not of your making. I'm sure you are completely unaware of the damage your son's business has done, and indeed is still doing, to the delicate ecology of that area.'

Bert said nothing, so Ethan went on. 'I just think it's a bit unfair, you being the innocent party and your son disappearing in such unpleasant circumstances.'

Tobacco smoke filled the airless room as Bedlow continued trying to gull the old man. He harped on the point that the cost of cleaning up the scrapyard would be astronomical and, unless it was done soon, could entail serious consequences. To hear him talk, you'd have thought his son had been storing plutonium in cardboard boxes, thought Bert, but he said nothing. Occasionally he rolled another cigarette just to top up the atmosphere, which was currently that of a 1950s pub at closing time.

When he finally ran out of steam Bert asked, 'How much?'

Dry of throat and faint from second-hand smoke, Bedlow replied, 'Three thousand. Which, considering everything, is, I think, a generous offer'.

'Cash?' said Bert

'It could be arranged.'

'Drop me a line and we'll see, eh?'

Ethan Bedlow extracted his business card, placed it carefully on the mantel- piece and left, grateful to be out of the room and fairly sure he had made the deal. After all, the old boy was practically gaga and had probably never seen £3000 in his life. Those cigarettes, though. Well, at least his cleaning bill would be on the company.

When he arrived home, he left his jacket in the garage, but his wife still insisted he go straight up and shower.

'I don't know where you've been, darling,' she said, 'but you smell frightfully common.'

~~~

One Sunday a month, Mrs Spottiswood invited friends around for 'tea'. Tamika referred to them as 'the coven', but Galadriel didn't mind and sometimes even joined in. Today's gathering consisted of Mrs Spottiswood, hostess (pendulum and carrot cake), Carmel Petalingo (palm reading and cream sponge), Mrs Woody (tantric crochet and Dundee cake), and Lucy Driver (tea wine and local rumour). Doris had also been invited and brought a bottle of mead from her uncle and bread pudding from her mum.

At 5:30 the dining room table was blessed in the name of 'the all-knowing', which covered most points on the belief scale and, unlike the Ouija board, caused no squabbling. Last month there had been a great deal of unpleasantness when Mrs Grindle had accused Beryl Creddit of manipulating the glass (not to mention bringing a shop-bought cake that was well past its 'best before' date). Today, once the spirits had been evoked, the harmonies aligned, and readings of one sort and another had taken place, gossip and speculation were exchanged. Galadriel wasn't there, so she was the subject of both. The general consensus was that her aura was looking much better of late.

'Far less of an imbalance,' said Carmel, who was recognised as the expert in this field. 'Less pink than there has been, and I've even seen some indigo breaking through.'

'Some orange would be a good sign' said Mrs Spottiswood (who also fancied herself an authority on auras). 'I haven't seen any yet, but we can hope.'

'Do you think it's on account of Tamika being more in charge?' ventured Doris, who hoped to have an aura of her own one day.

Lucy Driver said the word around town was that since Geoff Bendix had done a runner, Dai Griffiths had stepped in and was dipping his wick. She was disabused of that idea immediately by both Mrs Spottiswood and Carmel. But they all agreed there were still some bad vibes to be got rid of before the true spiritual harmony that Grey Havens was known for could be restored.

'After all, Mrs Meldrum died just a few yards from where we're sitting,' said Mrs Spottiswood. Then she lowered her voice and added, 'Her spirit may still require its settling.'

Doris made a bit of a fuss at this and had to be calmed down. She was told it was just a natural occurrence of the inexplicable, occult forces in need of balancing, and she wasn't to worry. She was well protected by those present and the powerful influences they wielded.

'In this world and the next, my dear,' said Lucy Driver, 'we women of the sacred paths do protect and serve, especially those like yourself who are virgins in the occult.'

That only caused further confusion for Doris, who had lately been enjoying the carnal attentions of Charlie Willow Walker.

'Samhain, then,' said Mrs Woody. 'You used to have such a good one here back when it was Rainbow Lodge. There was always a huge bonfire on the far side of the back lawn where they burned all the rubbish.'

'But Samhain's on Thursday,' said Mrs Spottiswood. 'That's just four days away. There's not much we can do in four days, is there? Besides, we mostly recycle everything now.'

Doris said her dad could provide plenty of wood pallets to burn.

'Yes,' said Carmel thoughtfully, 'Samhain. That might be just the thing provided we keep it small. Just the residents and a few good friends like yourselves.'

'Will we take our clothes off?' asked Doris, more in hope

than dread.

'No, dear' said Mrs Spottiswood. 'That is neither necessary nor wise. You have no idea how far sparks can fly and what they do when they get there.'

'We just need to organise the food and drink, then,' said Carmel. 'I'll put a note up in the common room asking for volunteers.'

On Monday Tamika was ambushed by Doris, Carmel, and Mrs Spottiswood and made to see how much a Samhain celebration was needed. With Tamika on board, it was easy to convince Galadriel. A patch of land at one end of the lawn was approved, and Doris's dad was commissioned to bring in the pallets. Desmond was asked to help with the bonfire and tackled the project with his usual gusto. He broke up the old pallets and added wood from around the yard and anywhere else he could get it. Galadriel watched the pile grow and actually became a little excited.

There would be plenty of good things to eat, too. Nearly everyone had signed up for something and a menu had now been posted. In fancy lettering it read:

*Starter – Prawn Cocktail*
*(Mrs Spottiswood)*

*Main Course – Mushroom Stroganoff*
*(Janet Browne)*

*Salads and Sides*
*(Galadriel and Tamika)*

*Puddings – Sherry Trifle (Doris's Mum)
and Fruit Crumble (Carmel)*

*Local Cheese & Biscuits
(Major Dennis)*

Granny did not take part in planning the Samhain celebrations, but she followed them with great interest. She was as patient as the next psychopath, but the thought that Miss Browne might betray her to the others (or possibly already had) preyed continuously on what was left of her mind. She had therefore made a certain decision and deemed its consequences both necessary and worthwhile. Careful eavesdropping had revealed that the bonfire would be the main event, followed by the meal. All she needed was the opportunity to add her own very special ingredient to the feast. It would only take a moment, but she had to make sure everyone would be out of the kitchen. After a little thought, she got her purse and headed into town. Money was no object now; it was time she couldn't buy.

Over the next few days, plans were pursued, provisions were procured, and decorations of a suitable kind were made. Even Bert got caught up in the excitement and asked Carmel at breakfast one morning if she were going to get her kit off for a bit of the old pagan prancing. 'Only if you do', was her reply. Bert laughed and said twenty years ago he might have, but not now, it would frighten the horses. He had tried to persuade Tamika to allow Daisy to join in the fun, but that idea had been met with a definite refusal. Those who understand these things know that beneath the dressing up and the drunkenness, a more sombre rite is being observed. Samhain is the feast of the dead, and events set in motion during this time have a life of their own. What goes around comes around, and it's during Samhain that what has gone around is most likely to find its way back.

~~~

Granny had found her way to Taunton where she had explained to a very nice man in a very special shop that she wanted a supply of their very best fireworks.

'They're for my grandson, to celebrate his twenty-first birthday,' she said, 'so I want lots of sparkly things that go whoosh!'

He smiled at the sweet old lady and provided just that. They weren't cheap, but there were plenty of them.

Upon her return to Grey Havens, Granny found Desmond in the garden, working away on things combustible. She took him a cup of tea and explained about the fireworks.

'I want to contribute something, but I don't want any fuss; they'll only tell me I shouldn't be spending my pension on such things. So, you have these as a gift from me and promise not to tell my friends I bought them, and we can all have a jolly time.'

Desmond was so touched by Granny's altruism that he offered her the pretty little bottle of mead Charlie Willow Walker had given him for fixing his car earlier in the week. He had told Desmond it was made from a special type of honey and was 'a bit lively', but no more than that. Granny liked sweet things, and, with a simpering smile, she accepted the gift. She told him she would drink his health with it during the bonfire.

~~~

On Thursday, the kitchen was taken over by Miss Browne and Doris from noon onwards. The first thing they did was sort through all the fungi Miss Browne had collected and dried since she'd come to Grey Havens. There were species that even Doris, a true country girl, had never dared to eat. But Miss Browne knew her stuff and happily explained everything to Doris in a kindly if somewhat schoolmistressy way. She said they were going to prepare mushroom stroganoff using a recipe given her by a famous French chef. Foreign didn't impress Doris much, but the way Miss Browne went about things did, so she kept her mouth shut and did what she was told.

Miss Browne had chosen the largest pan Galadriel possessed, a massive enamel stock pot. Soon an appetising smell pervaded the kitchen.

Mrs Spottiswood came in, sniffed the air, and said, 'That smells delicious, I can't wait to try it. I'll leave preparing my starter till the last minute. You don't want me under your feet right now.'

She had driven to a nearby Waitrose where they had a fish counter and bought a couple dozen really big prawns. Prawn cocktail might be a bit passé, but hers would be a triumph of seafood, crisp lettuce, and Marie Rose sauce.

The dining room was taken over by Mrs Spottiswood, who decorated it with ivy and green boughs from the garden. The table was laid by Carmel, who placed some really big candles around a centre decoration of a ram's skull, complete with horns. Unfortunately, the skull was removed by Miss Browne, who said there was no way she was going to look at that dreadful thing while she ate. Besides, the centre of the table would be taken up with her huge pot of mushroom stroganoff.

The Major was in charge of drinks. Charlie Willow Walker

had promised to deliver cider and beer, but of course he didn't. (He didn't even turn up. This was a disappointment only to Doris, but not for long as she took consolation in flirting with Desmond, who seemed a much more reliable young man.) The Major and Tamika went into town and came back with a barrel of scrumpy and several crates of beer, a couple bottles each of Scotch and gin, plus a cheap Spanish brandy.

Dusk fell. Desmond lit the bonfire and flames soared upwards. Outriders of sparks shone brightly for a moment and then died. There was no singing or dancing, just flames in the night in which the faces of the departed could be seen by those who had lost loved ones.

Mrs Spottiswood remembered her silly, stuffy, kind husband. They had been the best of friends until the day he died.

Carmel saw the face of her father. Such a rogue, such a charmer, such a loving man, even if he couldn't keep his hands off the dancers. But very kind to his only daughter.

Major Dennis stood upright, almost to attention, as if reviewing the troops he had led so long ago.

Bert had been a soldier once, too, until he had deserted. He had seen war and tasted its bitter fruits, had seen men die and felt the warmth of their blood on his uniform. He saw their faces but couldn't remember their names. He hobbled over and stood next to Major Dennis, an old soldier who had not run away. The Major seemed to understand his need and recited the timeless words in a low voice:

> *They shall grow not old, as we that are left grow old:*
> *Age shall not weary them, nor the years condemn.*
> *At the going down of the sun and in the morning,*
> *We will remember them.*

Desmond sensed that now was the time. He made his way discreetly to the place where he had set up all the pyrotechnic delights and began to light the fuses. Flowers of fire exploded over Grey Havens. After the initial jump of surprise, there were all the oohs and aahs that always accompany such things. No one asked where the fireworks had come from, they just enjoyed the spectacle. It changed the mood from thoughts of the departed to reminiscing about Guy Fawkes parties from their childhoods.

The fireworks were a signal to Granny to go about her business. She had been sitting in a garden chair on the patio and could see that everyone was now outside. She went up to her room, put on a pair of rubber gloves, and took her last bottle of aconite tincture from its hiding place. She had no expectation of getting away with this crime, but it would be worth it to watch them all die. She'd murdered her way to fame once before and would do it again. No longer the insignificant little old lady talked down to by shop assistants and treated like an imbecile by anyone under forty. Sod them! Sod them all, especially that clever busybody Miss Browne. If she couldn't die alone, then she would die with plenty of company.

In the kitchen, Granny poured the bottle of poison into the simmering pot and gave it a bit of a stir. "Bit of a stir!", she thought. The Old Bill will be in a bit of a stir when they see what this lot does to the fucking halfwits in this place. She threw the empty bottle and her rubber gloves in the trash. There was no point in trying to hide anything now (she had disassembled her equipment and moved it from the attic to her locked wardrobe, but that was more from ingrained habits of neatness than anything else.) She went to the lounge and settled in her accustomed armchair, from which she could see right into the dining room. Time for a little drink, she thought. Killing people is thirsty work! She opened the small, ornate bottle given to her by Desmond and poured its contents into a teacup. She hadn't felt so alive in years. This was something special. Not quite as thrilling as the first time with the family, but a lot less work than doing away with old ladies. And afterward, the state could cherish her old bones and pay for her living.

Eventually everyone meandered into the dining room, where the Major handed out drinks, and Desmond was congratulated on a job well done. The bonfire still burned, but it was a mere glow at the end of the garden now, just visible from the French windows. The candles were lit, the lights were lowered, and everyone sat down. In accordance with tradition, there was one empty place for those who had 'crossed over'. Conversation flowed as alcohol relaxed and rejuvenated the party. Mrs Spottiswood went to the kitchen to assemble the starter, and Miss Browne followed her for one last stir of the pot, her *pièce de résistance*, nature's earthy bounty glorified in a luscious gravy.

Mrs Spottiswood assembled her ingredients at one end of the kitchen table. She hadn't realised she'd have to shell the prawns until she took them out of the bag. She quickly got to work on them.

Miss Browne laid a large tea towel on her end of the table in preparation for transferring the huge pot of stroganoff from the cooker. The handles were extremely hot, and she wrapped two tea towels around them just to be on the safe side.

Bast, unobserved, wandered into the kitchen and

immediately detected the prawns. He adored prawns and sometimes, as a treat Galadriel would share hers with him. Full of anticipation, he leapt up onto the table. Mrs Spottiswood, caught off guard, cursed and shoved him to the other side of the table. Bast was now confused, angry, and off balance. Then something came silently and quickly up behind him. He always believed the 'fight' came before 'flight' and turning, he lashed out with his razor-sharp claws. They laid open the back of one of Miss Browne's hands. Hands which were tightly gripping the handle of an enormous, simmering pot of mushroom stroganoff. Miss Browne screamed. Bast having dished out a bit of fight, turned to flight and made his escape via her stockinged leg, slowing his descent by a controlled use of his claws. Miss Browne was made of stern stuff, but there is only so much a body can take. She let go of the pot.

There was no rescuing the stroganoff. Once the simmering pot landed the contents had all run glistening and steaming through the old rush mat into myriad crevices in the flagstones. Miss Browne's language was, as the Major said afterwards, something special. He hadn't heard swearing like it in years. Even Bert was impressed. By some miracle she wasn't scalded, just shaken, and extremely upset by the loss of her glorious creation. After all the work and preparation, she had put into it and that it was the main course of the meal, it was too much for her. She said she would just sit in the garden for a bit. The Major poured a large whisky and took it out after her. He said nothing, just handed it to Mrs Browne, along with a clean white hanky to cover the wound in her hand.

Tamika and Galadriel cleared up the mess. Neither was tempted to dip a finger into the remains of the stroganoff for a taste as the kitchen floor was fairly muddy and extremely catty. Out came the mop and bucket and all the kitchen towel they could lay their rubber-gloved hands on.

Meanwhile, Granny was still sitting in the common room. Charlie's 'lively' mead had certainly made her world a more interesting place. She clutched her knitting bag with whitened knuckles as, behind her eyes, elderly dead bodies bobbed in foaming bathwater. Tendrils of hair floated amid the bubbles like grey, white, and purple seaweed. Voices in her head cried, sobbed and pleaded, one in a childish lisp, others in various quavering tones.

Suddenly she got to her feet and dropped every vestige of Granny Toogood along with her knitting. Upright and in icy control, Mildred Thresh walked into the dining room. Unfortunately, everyone was still alive. None of them were even writhing in anguish. She went through to the kitchen and saw Tamika and Galadriel, heads down, mopping up the remains of the stroganoff, the empty pot already soaking in the sink.

It was over. All her efforts wasted. Her last chance at fame and revenge was gone, destroyed by these New Age imbeciles and their infuriating luck. Her mind fizzing with the effects of the spiked mead, Mildred was like an engine running out of control. She was a missile guided by hate, and with only one target.

'Where's Miss Browne?' she asked through clenched teeth.

Without looking up, her mind focussed on reaching a particularly slimy mushroom under the cooker, Galadriel said, 'She's in the garden'.

Mildred quietly took a big kitchen knife off the draining

board and left through the back door. She moved quickly across the lawn and into the trees, the long grass wetting her skinny legs in their thick, sensible stockings. She could see her target, quite alone, sitting under the canopy of the apple trees, bent as if in prayer. Good. She would walk slowly and calmly to where Miss Browne was sitting and disembowel her. She would spill her guts with one great slash from groin to ribcage.

Mildred caught movement in the corner of her eye. That fucking Spottiswood woman had left the dining room and was striding towards the small, seated figure. No! She would not be thwarted again! She sprinted between the trees, determined to reach Miss Browne first. She carried the knife well out in front of her with the point ready to stab in low and rip upwards. Just as she became certain she would win the race, her path crossed that of another killer running through the tall grass. Bast was chasing a rabbit. He shot between her legs, causing her to stumble. She tried to right herself, but the wet folds of her skirt tripped her up and she fell. The knife went in under her chin and buried itself up to the hilt.

What had gone around for so long had come around at last. As consciousness drained away along with her life's blood, what went around had finally come around. And in her head her screams stretched out into infinity.

Back in the dining room, everyone agreed the feast must continue despite the loss of the stroganoff. After all, there was lots of other food, and drink aplenty. Tamika always had something on standby in the freezer so they ate their starter and many of the other good things while a vegetable stew heated up the oven. It was an evening they would all remember, for many reasons.

A Glastonbury Tale

*Chapter 17*

There is a saying that guests, like fish, begin to stink after three days. Other things begin to stink even sooner. Granny's body was discovered on the second day after her death by Major Dennis, who recognised the smell at once as he made a search of the orchard.

That the woman had been missing for two days was a source of embarrassment to Tamika, who prided herself on knowing the whereabouts of all Grey Havens' inhabitants. But, after all, as Mrs Spottiswood pointed out, 'the dear lady kept herself so much to herself so much of the time.'

Even so, it was all a bit much when her body was found in the long grass near the apple orchard. Especially as, when the police turned her over, it was clear that not only was her death extremely unnatural, but some animal had been chewing bits off her. Everybody said, 'foxes' but they all (except Galadriel) thought 'Bast'.

As Major Dennis put it, 'Nature raw in tooth and claw, what?'

The body was taken away and the orchard was festooned with police tape. Once again, Doyle conducted seemingly endless interviews with the residents of Grey Havens with the dubious assistance of PC Pugh. It was all very distressing, though not as distressing as what was eventually found in her wardrobe when they searched her room. The door was locked, but it had been easy enough to force. A brief examination of the Gladstone bag was enough to tell DS Doyle there was more to the story than he could have imagined.

Doyle returned to Grey Havens a few days later, having phoned Tamika first and asked if it was convenient to have what he described as a chat with them all. Not an interview or anything dreadfully official, just a chat. Everyone gathered in the dining room and drank tea, very civilised and polite, but there was an undeniable tension in the air. The first thing he told them was that Granny Toogood's death was unquestionably accidental, after which everyone visibly relaxed. The second thing he told them was that she was not Granny Toogood. Then he gave them as much of her history as the police had been able to work out so far.

'So, Granny Toogood was really Mildred Thresh?' asked Galadriel.

'Yes, no question about that. Her fingerprints are on file. But why she was running around the garden with a bloody great carving knife on the night of your shindig is, frankly, a mystery we may never solve.'

When Doyle left, Tamika walked him out to his car. 'Speaking of mysteries,' she said, 'it's hard to believe Geoff Bendix hasn't turned up after all this time. Do you think he's still alive?'

'Yes', said Doyle, 'I imagine he's just lying very low somewhere.'

'Are you still looking for him?'

'No, I've been taken off that case. DI Franks, my guvnor, wanted a new team on it. Said I was getting nowhere, and I should give some other bugger a chance.'

Hearing the unhappy note in his voice, Tamika peered at him closely. 'You look tired,' she said.

'The truth is I'm being run ragged on a lot of small, stupid jobs a probationer could do. Shop lifters, petty thefts, stuff like that.' He didn't mention all the surveillance work he'd been doing on his own time.

Seeing she looked concerned, he gave her a smile. 'But the overtime's good, so that's something.' And with a wave, he drove off.

~~~

The strange death of the person now known to be Mildred Thresh created a lot of publicity. Glastonbury was not averse to publicity, but anything that threatened the town's famous wellbeing and harmony was taken seriously. Three covens and a convocation of druids offered to rid Grey Havens of its negative energies, and one 'red top' tabloid reported the death had taken place in a sacred grove that was a place of blood sacrifice in ancient times.

Tamika was worried. Not about the publicity, but about Bert. His cough had got worse, but he refused to see a doctor.

'I'm all right girl, just a bit of the bronchials. Get me some more of that jollop from the chemist and pass me my fags, will you?'

She did the one but not the other and he was too weak to get up and fetch the tobacco himself. Major Dennis had become a frequent visitor to Bert since the night of the bonfire. They raked over the ashes of their lives together with no judgement on either side. There was always a whisky bottle on the table and clouds of pipe and cigarette smoke in the room. Tamika liked to see Bert talking with someone other than herself or Auntie Grace, but she wasn't happy about the amount of smoking they did.

'I wish he'd stop smoking those bloody cigarettes,' she told the Major one day when they were alone in the kitchen. 'He knows they make him cough.' She didn't add 'and so does your ruddy pipe,' but it was in her mind.

'We all go to hell in a handcart of our own making,' was his response. Then he added, 'He's very fond of you, you know. Not an easy man to get close to, but I can tell you this: he may not always have been good, but he was always honourable.' And on that, the Major lit his pipe and left the kitchen.

The next morning, when Tamika came in with his breakfast, Bert said he wasn't hungry and would stay in bed for a bit. That wasn't unusual these days, so she just made sure his tea was within reach and his tobacco tin was not. But when she checked on him later, his face was white and covered in sweat. She phoned for an ambulance and then settled on the bed to wait with him.

Bert was rushed to the nearest A&E unit, some twelve miles away in Yeovil. Tamika went with him. The paramedic told her he'd had a heart attack and probably a pulmonary embolism but tried to reassure her that her father would be fine. Bert was barely conscious. At the hospital various tubes were inserted and a lot of other procedures were carried out. It was nearly ten by the times she left, but at least the doctors said he was stable.

The next morning Tamika returned to the hospital with a few of Bert's things and a card signed by everyone in the house. He was awake and looked better than he had the day before and she was pleased to see he was being well cared for. She visited him again that afternoon and took in a huge card from Daisy, which really seemed to please him. She was told she could spend as much time with her 'dad' as she wished, but despite the cheery optimism of the nursing staff, she knew he was very ill, especially when they moved him to a side ward next to the nursing station.

Tamika had just given Daisy her breakfast on Sunday when the phone rang. It was the hospital to say her father had taken a turn for the worse and she'd better come as quickly as possible. The journey seemed to take forever, but eventually she reached his bedside. A doctor was gently tending the frail figure under the sheet. The small room had just the one bed and a few machines measuring Bert's life in blinking lights. She took his hand and it felt like a bag of twigs, the skin thin, mottled, and heavily scarred. She lifted it to her lips and kissed it. She sat holding his hand for what seemed like hours, her arm stiff and uncomfortable. Tamika had never been religious, but she wished she was now so she could call on some god, ancient or modern, to make her vigil less lonely. Finally, Bert opened his eyes, turned his head, and looked at her. He gave her a smile and bells started ringing, people rushed in, and she moved out of the way to let the medical team do what they could. As she stood outside the room, she imagined she could hear the roar of a distant crowd and the voice of a referee: ten, nine, eight, seven—Tamika knew Bert would not rise to his feet before the end of the count this time. He had fought his last fight and death was the victor.

The worst part was trying to explain the inexplicable to Daisy, but Auntie Grace and the Jamaican traditions of Nine

Night were a great help with that. With the focus on celebrating Bert's life with food, music, dancing, and stories, it wasn't hard to keep Daisy from dwelling too much on his absence.

Over the next few days, Tamika endeavoured to expend her grief in activity, which helped her to be more cheerful for Daisy in the evenings. She cleaned out the room in which the woman she still thought of as Granny Toogood had lived. Bundles of clothes went to a charity shop, but not one in Glastonbury. Then she and Desmond and Galadriel burned the rest of her possessions, including the knitting bag. Galadriel said how strange it was that they had lit the flames to the old gods on this same site barely a week ago.

Mrs Danvers was saddened to hear of Bert's death, but she was a professional and soon had all the official and legal aspects of his passing well in hand. Tamika was, in modest terms, a rich woman. She didn't feel it, though. She felt lost, bereaved, and extremely tired. Major Dennis was a tower of strength and accompanied her to do all the dire registrations. He knew the ropes, he said, and two pairs of hands on them were better than one.

Doyle had called on Tamika, firstly to offer his condolences, and secondly to ask if he might come to the funeral. Tamika guessed why but told him he would be welcome. She had placed a memorial notice in the local papers. It was short and sweet, just giving Bert's birth and death dates together with details of the funeral and the fact that he would be missed. The notice was seen by Mr Smart who, like Doyle, thought this might just drive Geoff Bendix out of cover. It was uncanny the way no sign of him had ever been found, and Smart had stopped trying to contact Crabbe, who seemed to have completely vanished without even having been paid. The police hedged their bets by having the notice placed in local papers all over the West Country and South Wales.

On the ninth day after Bert's passing, Tamika stripped and cleaned his room until all that was left was the faint smell of his hand-rolled cigarettes. Desmond helped her turn Bert's mattress to the wall so he wouldn't forget to go to heaven that night, then accompanied her home for the final and most lavish celebration of the nine. Auntie Grace cooked all of Bert's favourite dishes and Daisy was allowed to stay up until midnight when her adopted Grandad's soul would stop by for a final farewell. Being 'allowed' is not the same as being 'able', however, and she fell asleep in Desmond's arms a little before 10:00. At 12:00 the traditional music ceased and the opening bars of the theme from Star Wars suddenly crashed out. Afterwards, Tamika explained that Bert always reckoned Mohamed Ali (or Cassius Clay, as he insisted on calling him) had been the best boxer ever, and he had used the Star Wars theme as his entrance music.

'What was good enough for Mohamed Ali's entrance,' she said, laughing and crying at the same time, is good enough for Bert's exit.'

The next day, suffering from the effects of too much rum and not enough sleep, Tamika stood with the undertaker as the party from Grey Havens arrived at the crematorium. Major Dennis looked smart in his green blazer and beret, his ruddy face matching the red stripe in his regimental tie. The women, apart from Miss Browne, were dressed in bright clothes and adorned with the usual cascades of beads and occult jewellery that tinkled as they moved. Apart from a posy from Daisy, there were no other flowers. The service was short and not at all religious. The Major gave a brief address and that was that, for which Tamika was extremely grateful.

Doyle didn't attend the service itself. He arrived nearly an hour before it was due to start and parked his nondescript car in a row marked for 'staff only' right at the back of the car park. It was a spot from which he could see everything, and soon a familiar grey Volvo cruised in and parked up in the public area, about twenty yards away. Doyle thought back to the conversation he had had not a week ago with a man in Liverpool. He had taken some finding and the search had to be done so gently it wouldn't have disturbed an insomniac mouse. Let alone those who were watching over a Provisional IRA grass now living in hiding. But one good turn deserved another and true to his word Seamus Daily told Doyle what he knew of Robert Smart. None of it surprised him, made him feel unclean even having this information, but didn't surprise him one little bit. Not long after the Volvo, a saloon purred in and parked in the section of the carpark dedicated to 'mourners' (Doyle knew this because it said so in big white letters on the tarmac). He knew this car as well, and the copper driving it, too. Well, there they all were. Now it was just a case of waiting to see if Geoff Bendix turned up. But he didn't.

~~~

As it happened, Geoff didn't learn of his father's death until several weeks later. He was using an old newspaper to start a fire and saw the notice put in by the police. He phoned Grey Havens and spoke with Tamika, not so much to enquire about his father's last days as his final effects.

'There's a solicitor dealing with all that,' she told him.

'Give me their number, then.'

'Do you need money?'

'Of course, I need bloody money, what do you think!'

'You'll have to come to Glastonbury to get it.'

'Tamika, if you knew half of the trouble I'm in you wouldn't say that. The police are only a fraction of my worries. I'm being pursued by a shark and if he finds me he'll take me apart. Literally.'

'Maybe you should give yourself up to the police, then.'

Geoff swore and nearly put the phone down.

Tamika asked, 'Well, they could protect you, couldn't they?'

'Probably not.'

She told him about DS Doyle. 'I'll talk to him for you.'

Geoff didn't like Tamika much, but he did trust her and if she thought this copper was okay, then he probably was. Probably. Maybe. Geoff squirmed between the rock and the hard place.

'You can meet him in the workshop at the scrapyard. It's been long enough so no one'll be watching it anymore, and besides, everyone knows it isn't your property now. Desmond's been using it to fix his appliances, but I'll make sure he's somewhere else when you come. Doyle's straight, that I can promise you, and he can come when he's off duty and explain your options to you. If you want me there as a witness, I will be, and that's the best I can do.'

She didn't relish the idea, but if that's what it took, so be it. After all, he was Bert's son. The least she could do was try.

For his part, Geoff was tired of living in limbo. Maybe this really could work. He'd offer Smart to this copper, but only if he were guaranteed witness protection.

'All right,' he said, 'just make sure you're there. If I'm going to be a hostage to fortune, so are you. This Friday. 10 a.m. You phone your copper and I'll call you back in a couple of hours.'

Doyle was surprised to hear from Tamika, and even more surprised when she told him about Geoff Bendix. He agreed to the meeting, however, and promised he would come alone. He certainly wouldn't tell anyone at the nick as he was no longer officially on the case, and he knew whatever he said could well end up in the wrong ears.

~~~

On Friday, Geoff arrived just after 7:00 a.m. and parked his car where he had left his Range Rover. He was not surprised to see that gone. The big double doors of the garage were unlocked, and he eased the left one open. Strange to be back. The same smells, the same mess. Well, not quite. There were more dishwashers and tumble dryers than before, and their associated parts were neatly placed on the bench along with Desmond's tools. The cavernous room was cold, but at least it was dry. He went into his office at the far end of the building. Back here it was really gloomy, which matched his mood precisely. He had no idea what sort of deal he would be able to cut with this Doyle. All he had to offer was testimony about Smart's loan sharking. Would that be enough if the cops still thought he'd killed Smart's bagman?

Doyle was at the scrapyard by 8:00. Or nearly there; he parked up at the side of the road some way away and waited to see Geoff arrive. At 9:00 he thought, 'Crafty bastard, he's already in there.' He drove into the yard and parked up alongside the garage. He entered slowly and carefully, stopping just inside the doorway.

'You there, Mr Bendix?' he called.

Geoff stuck his head out of his office.

'You must be Doyle,' he said. 'Come on in. I'm afraid the coffee machine's bust, the croissants haven't arrived, and we're fresh out of tea.'

Doyle went into the office. There was just enough light coming through the filthy windows to delineate the big desk, the filing cabinets, and the filthy old couch. He decided to remain standing. Even in this gloom, Doyle could see Geoff was tired. He had the look of a man almost at the end of his tether.

Doyle didn't bullshit; he told Geoff there was a charge against him as a possible accessory after the fact in the murder of one William Washington at a garage in the Meare Road.

Geoff started to explain, but Doyle put his hand up and said, 'I know, I know. Forensics went over the Range Rover. There was a bloodstained footprint in it that matched one at the crime scene, and it's clear from the position of the print that you didn't go very far into the room. It's not you we want, it's Mr Smart.

'You're welcome to him. But he's a nasty bastard and he'll have me if he can, and you, too, if you get in his way, so I hope you were careful setting this up.'

Doyle put his mind at rest, 'there's no way he can find out about this little chat and if you decide to come in with me, I'll tuck you away somewhere nice and safe.'

'If? You mean I have a choice?'

'I told Tamika I'd give you a choice,' said Doyle. 'Easy way or hard way, but you choose, not me.'

Meanwhile, Tamika, dressed in a heavy beige duffle coat, wellington boots, and a red woolly hat and carrying a cloth shopping bag containing a flask of coffee, three mugs, and a tin of biscuits, walked down the lane from Grey Havens into the yard. She didn't notice the Volvo parked at the junction nearby and wouldn't have recognised it if she had. The door to the garage was partially open and she stepped inside, walked a few feet in and stopped by the washing machines.

'Hello?' she called.

'Tamika!' said Doyle, nearly running out of the office. 'What the hell are you doing here?'

'I've brought you coffee,' she said, lifting up the bag and wondering why all the fuss.

Geoff had emerged from the office and was lighting a cigarette. He was no more than ten feet behind Doyle, who had now reached Tamika and was just standing there, gazing down into her dark brown eyes. The red hat seemed to make them glow. Doyle had an almost irresistible desire to kiss her. If he had done so, however, he wouldn't have seen Robert Smart step into the doorway and raise a sawn-off shotgun. Doyle grabbed Tamika and spun around, enveloping her with his body. Keeping his broad back between her and the gunman, he attempted to scramble behind one of Desmond's washing machines. Smart moved to his right for a better shot.

Tamika heard the blast and was immediately borne to the ground beneath Doyle, the two of them ending up almost under the work bench in a heap of cobwebs, metal filings, and other rubbish. Doyle was heavy and motionless, but with her head pinned against his chest, she could hear the faint beating of his heart. A piece of lead shot had clipped Tamika's forehead and dug a furrow up into her hair line. Like all scalp wounds, it bled profusely. She closed her eyes to keep the blood out of them.

Smart fired at Geoff as he began to run wildly towards his office. Somehow Bendix only ended up with a few pellets in his left leg, but this was enough to bring him to the floor, alternately crying in pain and pleading for mercy. Smart, completely at his ease, reached into his pocket for two more cartridges.

Behind him, a large man in a dark overcoat walked silently through the door. DI Franks briefly viewed the scene, then moved forward and bent down to examine Doyle. His left shoulder and arm were a mess. Noticing Tamika pinned beneath him, her face covered in blood, he thought, 'Oh dear. That complicates things.'

He stood and raised his arm in the direction of Robert Smart, who was serenely fitting cartridges into his shotgun. The heavy bullet from his revolver tore through Smart's back and out of his chest, showering Geoff, who lay at his feet, with gore. The gun was an old army issue Webley, unregistered, and one a copper from Northern Ireland might well have tucked away for emergencies. There were no prints on the cartridges or the gun because Franks was wearing thin rubber gloves. He would place the firearm in Doyle's hand and fire another round so forensics would have powder residue to find, and job done. Smart had simply become too difficult and dangerous to work with and besides, Franks was retiring soon. So, he had set his uniformed nark to keep an eye on Doyle until he had caught up with Bendix, which he was sure to do eventually, the stubborn bastard. Then he had let Smart know where they were. After that, it was simply a case of waiting out of sight until Smart killed Doyle and Bendix before taking Smart out. Shame about Tamika, but these things happen.

Franks headed over to where Smart's shotgun lay so he could finish Bendix off, then make sure Doyle and the woman were dead. Geoff watched him the way a mouse watches a snake, paralysed with fear. Franks had almost reached the motionless figure of Mr Smart when he suddenly disappeared into the floor.

After a split second of shock, Geoff got to his knees and crawled to the edge of the inspection pit. His ears were ringing from the sound of gunfire, but he strained them to listen for any movement below him. He heard none. With manic energy, dragging his injured leg, he hauled the heaviest things he could find to the pit side of the pit and tipped them in. Every now and then he'd stop and listen, then go back to throwing car batteries, washing machine parts, tools, and anything else he could lift into the hole. After about ten minutes of this, he went into his office, lay down on the manky couch, and passed out.

Doyle groaned and tried to move. Finally, with Tamika pushing, he managed to roll onto his uninjured side. She sat up and cradled his head in her lap. Looking up and seeing blood all over her face, he became agitated.

'It's only a graze. Just flesh, not bone. I'm okay, honestly,' she reassured him.

He looked relieved but was too weak to say anything. She reached gently into his jacket pocket and took out his mobile phone. There was a faint smile in his eyes as he looked up into hers. A drop of her blood splashed onto his chin.

At 10.58 a.m. on Friday, 29 November 1996, a 999 call was received and acted upon. It was an unusually clear and concise call. No hysterics, no rambling, just the location and the fact that a policeman had been shot.

As Tamika waited for help to come, she held Doyle tight and focussed on his shallow breathing.

'Stay with me,' she said softly.

His eyes were still on hers.

'Stay with me,' she said, louder and more firmly.

His eyes remained open, staring into hers.

*Epilogue*

Time passed and life moved on.

Doyle had left the police force, his pension quietly enhanced by an administration that chose to take a 'least said, soonest mended' view of the whole ugly business.

There had been one journey, a couple of months after Doyle had left hospital, to a registry office in Wells. There they were married in a short, official service, after which they returned to Grey Havens and did it all over again in true Glastonbury style. Daisy was the most beautiful flower girl anyone had ever seen, in a dress of silks, satins, and velvets Carmen had created for her. It even included a pair of fairy wings, but everybody agreed it was the bright yellow Wellington boots that really made it.

Auntie Grace moved to a bungalow nearby, and at Grey Havens a little building work created a new apartment on the top floor. The view across to the Tor was the best ever, said the inhabitant of a small bedroom filled with teddy bears and plush toys.

Doyle was kept busy with the extensive grounds to tend and all the maintenance the old house generated. There were even plans for an extension if the need for more room arose.

Once his little troubles were cleared up, Geoff Bendix was

given a couple thousand pounds to piss off and never come back, which suited him. Galadriel discovered specialist tours with likeminded people that seemed to focus on wellbeing and spiritual harmony via comfortable hotels in warm places. She liked the experience as much for enlightenment as for the homecoming and catching up with all the news. Her place on the 'staff' such as it was, was now taken up by a lovely Polish girl called Lena who endeared herself to the household by being a superb cook. She fitted in wonderfully.

And Paddy Doyle's aim to make the world a better place was played out now on a much smaller scale. His new life contained more love than he had ever had before from not just Tamika, but Daisy also. And they grew ever closer as a family as time drifted by. It was more than enough and sometimes he thought was a lot more than he deserved.

A major project that helped Doyle more than any other was clearing the scrapyard and demolishing the old shed. He, Desmond and 'Big Alfie' one of Doris's many brothers, worked together for weeks. He got fitter, bronzed under the sun, and buried his past under the rubble. He also learned to like cider, well some of it anyway. Earth poisoned by oils and waste was carted away and ponds created. Land was cleared and a small meadow sown with the wildflowers that would have been there before the motor car was ever dreamed of.

With the help of Joe, the dowser, and the local archaeological society, the ancient well was excavated. What was there was recorded and preserved. Then it was left in its small glade of ancient trees and anyone who wanted could visit. There was no charge.

Tamika and Paddy planted new trees and cosseted the old

ones and as the seasons rolled by, the land awoke and began to thrive under their careful attention and benign neglect and, of course their love.

Glastonbury Tor looked down upon it all, and it was magic.

### A Glastonbury tale – 8 March 2021

Bernard Pearson – a sort of biography.

Bernard Pearson was born in 1946. In his past he has been at times a soldier, village policeman, door to door salesman, potter, sculptor, and painter.

Some thirty odd – and indeed some were very odd – years ago he met Terry Pratchett. They became good friends, and much fun was had by the both of them. This resulted in some books, interesting Objet' d' art and a few million Discworld postage stamps.

Remembering Terry's remark that writing is the most fun anyone can have with their clothes on. That's what he does now.

He bore the trepidations of 'Lockdown' with a stoic calm due mostly to the regular intake of Gin and pipe tobacco. And of course, the ministrations and enduring patience of Isobel, his best friend of the last forty summers.

He lives in Wincanton, Somerset, which doesn't seem to mind.

Printed in Great Britain
by Amazon